CAN'T LOOK AWAY

ALSO BY DONNA COONER

Skinny

CAN'T LOOK AWAY

DONNA COONER

Point

FOR JAY

This book was originally published in hardcover by Point in 2014.

ISBN 978-0-545-42766-1

10 9 8 7 6 5 4 3 2 1   16 17 19 20

Printed in the U.S.A.   40
First printing 2016

Book design by Jeannine Riske

SensorOnline

ALLEGED DRUNK DRIVER KILLS PEDESTRIAN

Published on: August 23, 2:36:17 PM MDT

Boulder, CO — A suspected drunken driver struck and killed a young girl at a crosswalk in a popular pedestrian mall. Miranda Grey, 12, died at the scene. Police said the girl was crossing lawfully at the intersection, which had a traffic signal, when she was struck by a fast-moving car. An older sister, 15-year-old Torrey Grey, was at the scene, but was uninjured.

The driver, Steve Waters, 53, was ordered held on $2.5 million bail for investigation of vehicular homicide.

"On the Internet, you live forever. Everything you read could have happened today. Or last year. Or never."

—Torrey Grey, Beautystarz15

CHAPTER ONE

BEAT THE BLUES AND LEARN FRESH BEAUTY TIPS

In September, my parents moved me and my dead sister to Texas.

Today, just one week after the moving trucks left us here, my parents are going to put her ashes in the ground out in the middle of nowhere. The thought of it makes my stomach churn.

"Are you sure you don't want to come with us, Torrey?" my dad asks as he paces back and forth in front of the couch. My mom stares off into space, her hands clenched in her lap.

"I'm sure," I say. "I went to the funeral." And we all knew how that turned out. Pictures of my grieving face ended up on Instagrams everywhere. There was talk that a camera was even hidden in the huge spray of pink roses. They never found out for sure.

Mom seems to want to argue with me, and then just doesn't have the energy. Like she doesn't have the energy to eat dinner or brush out the tangles in her curly blond hair. She did, however, have the strength to keep going down to that corner at Pearl and 10th Street back in Colorado. My dad found her there, night after night, staring at that little pile of wilting flowers and teddy bears and holding handwritten cards from strangers.

"We all need a new start," my dad says now, looking at my mom. I know that part is about me, too. I can't really blame him. He's trying to fix things. That's what Dad does. That's why we're here in Texas, sitting on a couch the color of dead leaves and talking about putting what's left of my sister in the dirt.

Right after the funeral in Colorado, my parents discussed the move to Texas. Well, the truth is, my dad talked about it and my mom just stared at things like forks and lamps. I tried to not get in the way, and didn't say anything at all, even though the thought of moving away from Boulder was another thin layer of sadness pushed down on top of all the grief.

"It's just for a little while," Dad said. Like we'd come back again after a few months.

When my mother finally agreed to go, there was only one condition.

My sister, Miranda.

My dad, ever the planner, already thought of this and had an answer ready. "My family has a cemetery plot down in Huntsville. We can put her there and be close by."

The next day, Mom carefully rolled up the silver vase containing my sister's ashes into bubble wrap and placed it in a specially made travel box the funeral people gave us.

And just like that, even though it didn't make any sense to me, we all went to Texas. I didn't speak up because I didn't deserve to have an opinion.

I never knew you could bury ashes when people died. I thought you were supposed to keep them on the mantel or sprinkle them across the ocean. That's what they always did in the movies.

"There won't be anyone else there today. Right, Scott?" my mom asks my dad now in a quiet monotone. She talks like that a lot now. No one would guess she lectured to hundreds of biology students at the university in Colorado. She quit when Miranda was born and went back to teaching part-time when my sister went to kindergarten. Even so, she still had a wait list every semester of students wanting to get into her section. She was that good.

My dad nods and adds, "Just us and the funeral home people."

I can't give them the answer I know they want to hear. "I'm not going," I say again.

"It's okay." My dad stops still and looks down at my mom and me, huddled together on the couch. "You don't have to."

My relief is followed quickly by guilt. I bite my lower lip, holding back any chance of changing my mind. I can hear the disappointment in his voice, but it just seeps down and blends into all the other sadness until it is indistinguishable.

He sighs. "If you want to shut it all out, Torrey, that's your choice."

"Nothing is my choice anymore," I mumble, but I know he hears it by the way his jaw clenches.

"She can't stay here alone." My mom's voice is starting to rise.

My dad glances over at her, frowns. "She won't be by herself. Uncle Leo and Aunt Kim are coming over. They said they'd keep her company." My dad knew all along I wasn't going. He planned for it. I'm sixteen years old and need a babysitter. Even worse, the babysitters are some hick-a-billy relatives I've only met once, when I was eight. Great. But there's no sense in arguing. Not today.

"You're sure?" My mom's liquid blue eyes are pleading, but I'm not giving in. She can just add it to the long list of all my other failings and shortcomings.

"Yes," I say, firmly. It feels like I'll drown if I don't break away. I stand up. Her fingers cling to me, dropping off my shoulder only when I step out of their reach, but I know it's not me she really wants.

Later, I wave good-bye from the front door with a fake smile plastered on my face. I glance around to see if anyone's watching. Out of habit, I guess.

I go back inside, closing the door behind me and turning the lock. I don't know why I bother, because minutes after my parents drive off, I hear my uncle and aunt coming in the unlocked back door.

"Anybody home?" my uncle calls out.

"In here," I answer, and hope they stay in the kitchen, far away from me. Powering up my laptop, I sit down by the window in the big leather chair that looks just as old and shabby as the rest of this rental house. We don't have an Internet connection yet, so I make do with the only spot where I can catch the neighbors' unprotected wireless signal.

I lurk on Facebook first, scanning the postings and photos. I still have an account even though I haven't posted or commented since August.

Cody Davis and Zoe Williams are now friends.

Cody Davis wrote on Zoe Williams's wall. *Are you going to the party on Friday night?*

Cody Davis commented on Zoe Williams's photo. *Looking good.*

There's one photo that catches my attention, but I don't "like" it. It's a great picture of Zoe, but then she always looks good for the camera. The bright pink furry hat is the perfect complement to her olive complexion and her straight white smile. There is no sign of that horrible overbite she had until sixth grade. Kids called her "rabbit face" until I punched them hard in the arm and they stopped. In the Facebook photo, she's waving from a wooden bridge. Looks like Vail in the background. When Mrs. Timbley asked me in the seventh grade what I wanted to be when I grew up and I said "famous," everybody but Zoe laughed. She knew I was serious and had been my best friend and favorite accessory ever since.

There is another new picture posted and I definitely don't like this one. In this photo, Zoe's wearing a purple lace sheath dress and black pumps. The tall blond boy in the picture has his arm draped around her shoulders. His smile is crooked with the right side just a little higher than the left and, even though I can't see them in the picture, I know there are tiny little crinkles around his blue eyes. He's wearing a suit. I'm more used to seeing him in jeans and hiking boots, or maybe his lacrosse uniform. I've only seen him dressed in a suit once before. At my sister's funeral.

Cody Davis is in a relationship with Zoe Williams.

Boom. There it is. Curling my fingers into my palm, I dig my nails into the soft skin. Life is going on without me. As though I never existed.

Hurriedly, I click over to YouTube and log on to my video channel. I feel the now familiar rush at the still of my face on the screen, and I study my well-known username: Beautystarz15. My adrenaline spikes when I see the subscriber count. Three hundred thousand of my closest Internet friends all waiting anxiously for my next post.

They'll have to wait a little longer.

I select the most popular video, already viewed more than a hundred thousand times. In it, Zoe and I are sitting on my bed in my pink-walled room, surrounded by Forever 21 and Anthropologie bags. I'm wearing the Dior sunglasses I picked out that day from a clearance rack, and my dark, thick hair is perfectly straight-ironed.

Zoe says it's my blue eyes combined with the dark hair that really makes my face pop on screen. She's probably right, but I figure I look like the popular girls at any high school. Tall, but not too tall. Thin, but not too skinny. I think that's why the vlog gets so many hits — I'm approachable. Like a new best friend who tells you what to wear and how to look good wearing it.

"After all, everyone deserves to see the fruits of our shopping trips and not have to ask where we bought stuff," Zoe had said that day, but only to me, because we weren't filming yet. "It's really a win-win."

"You're a snob," I told her. "That's exactly the kind of attitude that comes across on-screen. You have to be *likable*."

"You're one to talk," Zoe said, grinning at me, and then added, "you just hide it better than I do."

But none of the thousands of people who viewed this clip will ever know about that conversation. It took place before I hit RECORD on my laptop. They only see what's here.

I wait while the clip slowly loads. My face is frozen on the screen, then I come to life. Zoe is by my side and looking at me, just like we practiced a million times.

"So normally I would say floral jeans are going to make you look huge," I say, tilting my head slightly toward the left for the better angle. "But these skinny jeans by Free People I bought today at Nordstrom are perfect to make long legs look even longer."

I set down the jeans, and then pick up a purple jacket off the bed and hold it out toward the camera. "And if you really want to turn some heads, rock this fun faux fur with those jeans."

"Or go way edgier with Sam Edelman leopard-print booties and leather leggings," Zoe says, reaching down to grab my foot and pull it up into the frame. I scream and topple back onto the bedspread. Zoe collapses in a fit of giggles.

The image freezes and a spinning ball covers Zoe's laughing face. The Internet connection is too slow for video. I shut down the computer and sit for a minute staring at the black screen. Colorado seems a long way away. I reach for my phone in my pocket and then remember the battery is dead. It's the fifth time I've tried to use my phone since lunch. I feel lost without it. The charger disappeared somewhere in the move and it's driving me crazy. Maybe I'll ask Dad to take me to the Apple store when he gets back.

The sound of dishes clattering reminds me I'm not alone. But Aunt Kim stays in the kitchen, letting me be. Uncle Leo isn't quite so intuitive. He comes out to the family room and plops down in the chair next to me like he belongs there. He's sort of like Humpty Dumpty with a big silver Texas-shaped belt buckle planted right in the middle of his stomach. And he's a talker. Joy.

"Good thing this house right across the street from us was empty. I know your dad wanted to be near family. It's not what you're used to, but it's okay for now, right?"

I don't answer, staring at him with a look that usually makes people uncomfortable, but he just keeps talking.

"The school here is great. They've only been back in classes for a couple of weeks, so you won't have missed all that much. You're going to like it fine."

The chair gives a big squeak as he rocks back against the wall, his JCPenney shirt stretching tightly at the buttons. I wonder if it would be too rude to get my earbuds out and stuff them into my ears.

"You're sixteen, right?"

I just stare back at him. *What's it to you?*

"Do you have a car?"

I shake my head. "I don't have a license yet," I mumble, digging around in my Fossil bag for the earbuds. I don't add the fact that my birthday passed unnoticed weeks ago. Funeral arrangements make a trip to the DMV completely trivial. And seeing the crumpled front of a car that just hit my sister didn't make me eager to get behind the wheel. I especially don't want to talk about that.

"I've got just the thing." My uncle slaps his leg and I almost jump off the couch. "My daughter has her license. You remember your cousin, Raylene, right?"

I vaguely remember a skinny girl with big ears that I met at some relative's wedding when I was eight. We never had much contact with the Texas side of my dad's family before. Now we're practically living with them. I figure it's sort of like being in the witness protection program. No one is going to be looking for me here.

"I'm thinking maybe we can help each other out," Uncle Leo is saying.

I pause, with the earbuds ready to shut out his noise. He gets two, maybe three more sentences max, then I'm drowning him out.

"You don't want to be riding the bus to school, do you?"

Okay. Now he has my attention. There is no way I'd be caught dead in a school bus. Even one in Nowhereville, Texas.

"Raylene can drive you." He announces it like it's this huge present and I'm supposed to clap my hands in glee. "You'll be in the same grade anyway, so it'll help you get acquainted. She can introduce you to everyone."

How exactly is this helping *him* out? Does his daughter really need friends that bad? I give him a tight smile. Not only do I have to live across the street from these people, now I have to go to school with one of them.

"I'll go get her and you girls can make plans for Monday." He gets up out of the chair with a big groan at the effort and opens the front door. I hear him yelling from the porch.

Within minutes, a bleached-blond girl with a ponytail and a teased-up bump on the top of her head is standing in front of me. She holds a can of Diet Coke in one hand and looks me up and down, chomping away on a piece of gum, her big silver earrings jangling with the motion.

"I hear we're going to be in the same class."

I know she's heard a whole lot more about me, but she's restraining herself. Barely. Someone must have given her a good talk about it before I arrived but, honestly, I don't have much hope she is going to hold out very long. She takes a big swig of the drink, but doesn't stop staring at me. I notice for the first time there are little tacky daisies painted on each of her fingernails. This is evidently what I have to look forward to.

"Do you have a charger?" I ask.

She stares at me, still chewing away on her gum, like I'm speaking another language.

"My phone is dead." I throw in one of my smiles, with dimples and a flash of straight white teeth, for extra emphasis. When I was a kid I used that grin when I needed another quarter for the pop machine or a ride home from school instead of taking the smelly bus. Later, I discovered it even worked with teachers for an extra point for the passing grade, and classmates for the right answers on their math homework.

Raylene blinks at the quick change of subject and stares at me dumbly. I feel like reaching out and shaking her.

"A phone?" I stand up and make a motion like I'm punching in numbers on a keypad. Finally, her face clears and she nods, reaching in her pocket to pull out an iPhone with a tacky pink glitter case.

"Can I use it?" I ask, but I'm already taking it from her hand. I give her a look to let her know she needs to back off and give me some privacy, but she doesn't budge.

I try not to roll my eyes as I text Zoe. *Call me on landline. Phone is dead.* I hit SEND and then realize she won't know who it's from so I add, *It's me, T.*

I hand it back to my cousin. "Thanks."

"No problem." Raylene suddenly grabs my shoulders and pulls me in toward her body. She is evidently not discouraged at all by my frozen, board-stiff response because she just keeps hugging and hugging and hugging.

When she finally releases me, she smiles from ear to ear and says, "That's what cousins are for."

I slide back down into my seat. For a minute, I feel a strange twinge of envy.

How does it feel to be so blissfully unaware of other people's opinions? Have I ever felt that way?

"I'll pick you up on Monday?" Raylene asks.

In only a few days, I'll be part of this new world — bling, cowboy boots, and all. I nod, weakly, and watch Raylene turn and practically skip out the front door. Taking me to school with her probably just increased her popularity by 100 percent.

I lean my head back and close my eyes. I want to think about fashion and Zoe, but I don't. My mind immediately goes to the one thing I never want to think about, but can't forget.

That day.

It's all still there, swirling around in my head, like a snow globe you shake up so you can watch the world inside go crazy.

It was my idea to go to the mall that afternoon. I had been planning a new mega Urban Outfitters haul, and I thought it'd be cool to do the video right there, steps away from the front door. Zoe had begged to be part of the vlog. Since the last one she'd appeared in had been so popular, I agreed.

I'd pleaded with my sister, Miranda, to come along to the mall. I had to promise to buy her the latest edition of some comic book about a green-skinned superhero named Miss

Martian. I needed Miranda to hold the camera and film me and Zoe, though Miranda didn't know that yet. I'd spring that on her once we were there.

Pearl Street is a four-block pedestrian mall in the downtown area of Boulder. I don't know who thought they should have an outdoor mall in Colorado, but it's a popular spot even when there's four inches of snow on the ground. That August day, any sign of cold weather was at least a month away, and the intense high-altitude sun brought out the back-to-school shoppers and summer tourists alike. With the foothills as a backdrop and the cloudless blue sky overhead, it was like a postcard photo. The people were busy, the shops expensive, the hanging baskets exploding with flowers, and a different street performer was on every corner.

I was concerned with not tripping over the foot of a clown twisting a yellow balloon into the shape of a giraffe. I stopped so suddenly in front of Urban Outfitters that the woman behind me, carrying the efforts of hours of shopping, stumbled into my back. She mumbled a totally insincere apology and then stepped around me with a glare.

Funny how I remember those little details.

Zoe was waiting for me to keep my promise and include her in the video. All I needed was for Miranda to film the action. Maybe zoom in and out a couple of times. That's all. A simple request. But we'd been arguing, and Miranda was not cooperating. She stood there in that crazy purple plaid hat with the furry flaps down over her ears, even though it wasn't nearly cold enough to wear something like that. Her arms were crossed stubbornly in front of her and she was yelling so loudly that people were craning their necks to see what was causing all the noise. I was mortified.

"This is stupid and you can't make me do it." Her eyes were as blue as the cloudless sky, the exact same shade as mine, but oh so angry.

Then she turned and walked away. A stiff, obstinate back marching through the endless rush of people carrying shopping bags and Starbucks cups. I thought she would eventually come back. Instead she stopped when she got to 10th Street and cupped her hands around her mouth. I remember the big planter boxes full of bright yellow marigolds right beside her.

Guilt is the color of marigolds.

Standing perfectly still in the midst of the crowd pushing and shoving around her, Miranda yelled one final thing. Her voice carried across the sidewalk. The last time I would ever hear it.

"I'm going home!"

No black thunderstorm gathered in the distance. No ominous music played in the background. No sense there was a car coming down the road half a mile away with a drunk driver behind the wheel.

Everything was fine.

And then it wasn't.

SensorOnline

TEEN BEAUTY GURU'S TRAGEDY

Published on: September 14, 6:03:24 PM MDT

Boulder, CO — Just weeks after being dealt the devastating blow of her sister's tragic death, Internet star Torrey Grey is facing even more heartache from cyberbullies who claim she is capitalizing on the tragedy.

For more than a year, Boulder, Colorado, native Torrey Grey, or Beautystarz15, as she is known online, has cultivated a loyal following on YouTube, offering young girls her advice on shopping and fashion. Grey shows off her purchases in homemade videos she posts online.

In a terrible turn of events, Grey's 12-year-old sister, Miranda, was killed by a drunk driver just steps away from where Grey was filming her latest video blog. Grey's fans were deeply upset at the shocking news, posting hundreds of comments to her Facebook and YouTube accounts.

As a result of the exposure, Grey's videos have been receiving more than 2 million views, and critics have claimed she is using this recent tragedy as a publicity tool to gain even more followers. Even though Grey has not posted a vlog since her sister's death, her YouTube stats are soaring, jumping 10,000 or more a day. The public can't seem to get enough of Torrey Grey.

"Get over the self-consciousness of talking in front of a camera and just try to be unique. Make videos that you are dying to watch." **—Torrey Grey, Beautystarz15**

CHAPTER TWO
"GET READY WITH ME EVERY DAY" MAKEUP TUTORIAL

I shut off my alarm and fall back onto the pillow with a groan. Out of habit, I reach for my phone, now fully charged with the found cord, and check the most recent Google Alerts on my name. Pages and pages of hits. Not as many as two weeks ago, but the story — *my* story — is still getting picked up and spreading.

I always wanted to be famous, but not in this viral sort of way. It's the kind of fame that is fleeting and faithless. There was that guy who helped land the rover on Mars who was famous for his haircut. Or that girl who sang a really bad song about a day of the week. Or sometimes people are momentarily famous because something so horrible — so unimaginable — happens that we just can't look away. Like the woman crying into her phone as she runs toward a school. Or a beauty vlogger who witnesses her sister's death.

Being pitiable is never an attractive quality.

Even though part of me doesn't want to, I click over to my YouTube page. It loads infuriatingly slowly and I wait impatiently for each screen shot to appear. I scroll down to the comments. There are so many that say *so sorry* and *thinking of you,* but then there are the others.

Strangers' comments wait on my phone, like tiny emotional landmines. Behind the screen that keeps them anonymous and cruel, they have the power to wound me. My total value is summarized in one or two casual sentences that no one would ever say in person.

Get a life and get out of the mall. All you care about is yourself.

Stop using your sister's death for your own fame. Is it worth it just for more subscribers?

It was your fault.

I close my eyes and take in the cut of criticism deep. Then I look back down. The next comment makes my whole body shake. It's about Miranda.

Poor girl. She was just in the wrong place at the wrong time.

What kind of stupid thing is that to say? How could being in the middle of a crosswalk on a sunny day be the wrong place for a twelve-year-old? There was a man making a balloon giraffe and a woman playing bongo drums. When is the right time for someone to die?

You don't know my sister. You don't know me.

But this isn't a conversation. I know that. Posting a response will only make it worse, so I cram the anger and hurt down inside.

I close YouTube and stare at my phone. I haven't heard from Zoe since I texted her. But she's just busy. It has absolutely nothing to do with her guilty conscience about Cody. Or at least that's what I tell myself. If I could talk to her, I'd tell her that, too. No boy is going to ruin our friendship, not even Cody Davis.

Zoe knew I had a crush on Cody all of freshman year before he actually asked me out. I loved his tall, blond good looks and the sound of his laugh, surprisingly loud and contagious. I felt so special that he'd chosen me. He told me I was beautiful all the time, but he did often add that I looked better with my hair down. He didn't like it in a ponytail. He thought my videos were boring, but he loved boasting to his friends about my online stats. Sometimes, when we were together, I wondered if Cody would still like me if I weren't so popular. Or if I wore my hair in a ponytail all the time.

Pushing back the covers, I swing my legs over the side of the bed. Time to face the inevitable. A school full of new viewers.

I pull the red T-shirt I slept in up over my head and drop it on the floor of my new blah bedroom. Several drawers in the big oak dresser are open with a couple of socks dangling out. Tennis shoes and a black Ugg boot keep a pair of jeans company on the floor. This mess used to drive my mom crazy. Now she doesn't seem to notice.

The closet is half the size of my one back in Colorado, and stuffed to the brim. I pick out a pair of cigarette jeans and a plain white T-shirt with a scoop neck, tucking in the front and leaving the back out. I layer on a blazer, but decide against the fringed scarf. Instead I accessorize with a long beaded chain pendant and silver earrings. Red ballet flats add a bright pop of color, but after I slip them on I can't seem to stop staring at them. I just want to tap my heels together and go back home to Colorado.

Home.

Don't even think about it.

Quickly I braid my hair, put on some eye shadow and a bit of liner, brush on a neutral lipstick. One quick spritz of hairspray, and I call it done. I figure I'll still be better dressed than half my classmates.

There's no sign of my mom in the kitchen, but a scribbled note in Dad's handwriting is on the table. *Got to get to the office. Good luck and have a great day at the new school! Love you.*

I notice the unplugged home phone on the countertop. My dad probably did it. My mom can't even make the connection right now between cords and phones. It's irritating, but at least it explains why Zoe hasn't called. As usual, she was just following my directions to call the landline. It's why she's such a good friend. She listens.

By the time I stuff a hastily made sandwich in my bag and eat half a banana, Raylene is at the curb blasting on the horn of a beat-up red Chevy Blazer.

"I'm coming," I yell back from the window over the kitchen sink. My mom's bedroom door stays closed even with the honking and the yelling.

Outside, I slide into the car and pull the door shut behind me. It doesn't close.

"You have to slam it really hard," Raylene says.

Classy. I slam it three more times until it finally shuts.

Raylene glances at me as she pulls out into the street. She's wearing chandelier earrings that hang almost to her shoulders, a pink tee, and a blue-jean miniskirt. It's not great, but it's not horrible. Until I glance down. Cowboy boots with embroidered hearts and flowers? Seriously?

Raylene enthusiastically turns a corner and something hard on the floorboard bangs up against my ankle.

"Ouch." I fumble around and come up with a silver tube. "What *is* this?"

"A baton. I'm trying out to be a twirler."

Twirler? Like throwing a silver tube up in the air and jumping around?

"Why?" I ask, because honestly I can't think of a reason why anyone would.

"Because around here nobody runs for the bathroom and the food stand at halftime. They stay to watch the band *and* the twirlers. It's like being on Broadway or something."

"Well, good luck with that," I say, putting the baton back on the floorboard. I rest one foot on top of it so it won't hit me again.

"Thanks." Raylene grins at me. I don't smile back.

"Are you okay? You look . . ." She pauses.

I flip the visor down and glance in the cracked mirror. My eyes are red and even the best cover-up doesn't hide the tired purple smudges underneath. In my darkened bedroom, I didn't notice. "I'm fine," I say.

I close my eyes and try to ignore the queasy feeling in my stomach. Raylene slams on the brakes so fast my head jerks forward, hitting the visor in front of me.

An image of a crumpled body in a crosswalk explodes into my mind. Memory ricochets against my closed lids. I quickly open my eyes to escape back into reality.

Don't think about that. Not now. Not ever.

"Sorry," Raylene says. She rolls down the window to wave at the woman crossing in front of us, walking a small Yorkshire terrier. "Hey, Mrs. Berry."

My head is pounding and I rub a spot above my right eye as though that's going to help. It doesn't. Raylene just keeps talking as we drive on. I realize it's about the woman we just saw.

"Mrs. Berry owns the Paxton Boutique down on the square. They sell a lot of different things, but are probably best known for Poo-Pourri."

Unfortunately, I don't think she's kidding.

"They even have a sign on the door that says *Poo-Pourri. Spray a little in the bowl and no one will ever know.* I think they sell it online, too. There's evidently a pretty big market for Poo-Pourri."

I blink at her a few times, then turn my attention back out the side window.

"Nice jacket." Raylene blurts out after only a block of silence.

Nice is not how I would describe my three-hundred-dollar Italian wool blazer from Abercrombie, but whatever.

"Thanks," I say, looking out the window. A few houses have pumpkins out on the doorsteps and fake spiderwebs strung from porches. It's the only sign of fall. The sun is brighter than expected and suddenly I worry the jacket is going to be too hot. I'll probably have to ditch it in some stinky locker before lunch.

"I saw the vlog when you bought it. Cool store." She pauses, and then adds, "It must be amazing to have hundreds of people watch your videos every day." It's the first time she's mentioned my vlog, and I can tell she's relieved not to be bottling it up anymore.

You have no idea what it's like. No one does.

There are comments . . . follows . . . likes . . . tweets . . . posts. People are talking about me out there and I need to see it. My fingers twitch, but I resist the constant urge to pull out my phone.

"More like thousands," I finally reply. *More like hundreds of thousands,* I think, but don't say.

"Wow. You're, like" — she pauses and stares over at me — "famous."

Fame is a peculiar thing. You have to be famous *for* something. Like singing or acting or modeling. None of those work for me. I can't carry a tune. The thespian crowd is way too low on the social ladder for me, and I'm not tall enough to be a model. Haul videos don't take any special talent. You basically go shopping and then show people what you bought. But the results can be amazing. My "talent" led to fans, followers, subscribers.

But what else did it lead to? My head throbs again.

Raylene is still looking at me and not the road.

"Squirrel!" I point. Thankfully, the squirrel does a quick U-turn and scampers back to the safety of the curb.

"Huh?" Raylene makes a confused sound, but at least her attention is back on driving. "You probably get recognized everywhere, right?" she asks.

"People don't expect to see me in real life. It takes them a little while to realize who I am."

"But I could tell everyone at school," Raylene says enthusiastically. I feel a rush of panic at the thought.

"I'm kind of trying to keep a low profile. I haven't had a chance to update my subscribers since . . ." My voice trails off.

"Oh, sure. No problem," Raylene says.

But it is a problem. My YouTube channel is supposed to be reserved for cheerful videos describing my latest shopping spree or my favorite eye shadow pick. How exactly am I supposed to talk about ribbed thigh-high socks in an engaging, bubbly voice now that everyone knows my sister is dead?

"When are you going back to Boulder?" Raylene asks. "Maybe you could pick up one of those jackets for me. We don't have any of those stores around here."

I bite my lip. "I'm not sure. We'll go back for the sentencing, but who knows when that will be."

Raylene swerves into the oncoming lane to pass a guy on a bike and my fingers tighten on the armrest. I don't realize

I'm holding my breath until we pull back into the lane in front of him.

Raylene frowns. "You're going to be there in the courtroom for the trial?"

"There's not going to be a trial," I say. "He pleaded guilty of DUI. But the district attorney said the family can make a victim impact statement when he's sentenced."

I don't want to think about *him,* but I do. A wild-haired man, rocking back and forth on the curb in handcuffs.

"What's a victim impact statement?" Raylene's question pulls me back to the present.

"We tell the judge how my sister's death has affected us. It's our chance to represent the victim's side of what happened." My voice is robotic, repeating the exact words the district attorney said. I wasn't sure what they meant then, and I'm still not sure.

Raylene stares at me in fascination. I have to point out the green light.

"I saw that one time on a repeat of *Law and Order.* I was bawling my eyes out. And you're going to be the one to do it?" Raylene's voice is full of awe. And for the first time, I realize that maybe I *should* be the one giving the statement.

"My mom's not exactly in any condition to talk in front of people," I say, thinking out loud. Am I seriously considering speaking in the courtroom? Maybe then my dad wouldn't think of me as self-centered, and my mom . . . my mom would just think of me. And everybody else would, too. Not in a mesmerized, feel-sorry-for-you way, but with respect. The idea seeps into my brain, whirling around with possibilities.

Making that statement in court might be exactly what I need to do.

"I don't think I could ever do anything like that," Raylene breathes.

I shrug, but feel better than I have in weeks. It reminds me of how I felt when I had over a thousand "likes" on my vlog about fishtail braiding within ten minutes of posting.

"Will there be reporters?" Raylene asks.

"Probably," I say. The coverage is guaranteed to be extensive. They would probably link to my videos. It will be touching and inspiring. A perfect comeback. I'll just have to be ready with a really cool vlog to post right afterward, when all the traffic peaks. My mind zooms in and out of the conversation with Raylene.

Then Raylene asks a question that smothers my enthusiasm.

"What are you going to say? You know. About your sister." Raylene pulls into a gravel parking lot full of late-model cars and pickup trucks.

The question rattles around in my brain unanswered. What *would* I say about my sister? It's strange how two people can live in the same house with the same parents, yet be so different.

"I'll have to think about it," I say, and just like that the past rewinds.

There are things that wait in the dark outside the boundaries of glimmer and shine. They slither around quietly in the shadows and breathe slowly just outside the limits of what others believe. When Miranda was six, she saw them.

I was ten, and oblivious.

Mom and Dad redecorated Miranda's room. It was mainly so she'd stay in it at night. She picked out everything from the bright yellow paint to the monkey decals dancing all over the walls. Bunk beds so she'd have a choice of where to sleep. There were green, leafy pillows and even a rope-swing chair in the corner. It was the most cheerful room on the planet. A place where any respectable monster would be embarrassed to hang out. A definite no-nightmare zone.

None of it mattered. The first morning after the big makeover, I found her curled up in a ball sleeping on the floor beside my bed. And it kept happening. Every single night. The routine was always the same. Mom would visit each bedroom, kiss us both good night, and whisper her signature tagline into our ears, "Love you to the moon." Every night we both answered, "And back again." Then one hour later, like clockwork, I'd hear the quiet knock on my door.

"Go to bed, Miranda," I hissed, trying not to wake up anybody else.

The door creaked open anyway. She stood there in the hallway, the darkness of the sleeping house behind her, her big blue eyes full of unshed tears.

"I'm scared," she'd say.

"Of what?" We had this conversation hundreds of times. Maybe thousands.

"I don't know," she'd say.

"There's nothing to be scared of," I'd say, and I believed it. Then.

"I'll just lie out here in the hall." She dropped to the carpet and curled into a ball, tucking her hands under her head for a pillow, her eyes open and watching me.

"Go back to bed, Miranda."

But she was stubborn, and eventually I'd give up. "Okay," I'd say, and she'd bound into my room.

"Thank you, Torrey," she whispered fervently, as if I'd just granted her asylum from some horrible fate. She climbed over me and wedged herself into the spot below the window against the wall, snuggling into the covers and blankets with a big sigh of satisfaction.

"Promise me you'll stay here all night," she murmured, blinking up at me, her eyes just like my own. It was the only physical trait we shared. Otherwise, people wouldn't even know we were sisters.

"Go to sleep," I muttered back. "It's just for this one night. Tomorrow you go back to your bed."

But she didn't. So finally, after the bajillionth time, I decided to take matters into my own hands. Even at ten years old, I was already an expert in manipulating Miranda. After all, I'd spent most of my life figuring out ways to get her to leave my stuff alone. When she was two and I was six, an enticing trail of stuffed animals placed along the hall would lead her right away from my room. When she was four and I was eight, I would leave open picture books strategically placed on the couch to keep her from interrupting my favorite television show.

It only took a little research and a silver bracelet I never wore. The salesclerk at Claire's said the tiny gray-colored stone that dangled from the silver chain was called a moonstone. It wasn't my style, because even then I knew what I liked, but it was 75 percent off and the name of the stone was catchy. Moonstone. So I spent my allowance and brought it home to put in my ballerina jewelry box.

When Miranda showed up at my bedroom door like clockwork that night, I didn't argue, but let her climb right into the bed beside me. Once she was settled into her spot, I pulled up the shades. The bright full moon lit up my bedroom like the light was turned on. I couldn't have planned it better.

"Next year you're going to second grade, right?"

She nodded, looking across the bed at me.

"Second graders," I said solemnly, "are very grown up. They aren't afraid to sleep in their own rooms."

Her bottom lip stuck out and began to quiver. She knew where this was going.

"Do you want to sleep in your own room?"

"Yes." But she didn't sound so sure.

"Then I'm going to help you," I said. "I'm going to give you some magic words. You can say them to yourself at night and it will keep you from being afraid. You'd like that, right?"

She nodded again.

"So here's the secret. You say these words every night." I put my hand over my heart and recited the words I'd made up earlier. "When the moon shines bright . . ."

"When the moon shines bright," she whispered after me.

"Your fears will be few."

"Your fears will be few," she said.

"And only sweet dreams," I said, "will come to you."

Miranda repeated it faithfully, her big blue eyes unblinking. It was a piece of cake.

"Now you say it," I said. "From the beginning."

"When the moon shines bright, your fears will be few." Her voice was quiet, but steady. "And only sweet dreams will come to you."

"Good." I smiled at her.

"But what if the moon isn't shining? Because sometimes it doesn't."

I slid my hand under my pillow. She sat up in the bed, her head tilted to one side. I pulled the bracelet out and held it up so she could see the sparkle of the tiny gray stone dangling in the moonlight.

"Ohh . . ." It made a great first impression.

"This is a moonstone," I said. "Some people say these special jewels are really rays of the moon captured in the rock."

Miranda reached out a tiny finger to touch it and the movement caused the light pouring in from the window to scatter across the wall.

"So I'm going to give you this very special bracelet. When you put it on, and say those magic words, you won't be afraid

to sleep in your own room anymore. Because you'll always have the moon with you."

Her eyes got even wider.

"You understand?"

She nodded. I fastened the bracelet around her tiny wrist. She grinned up at me in excitement, twisting her arm from side to side and watching the stone shimmer.

"When the moon shines bright, your fears will be few," she chanted softly, "and only sweet dreams will come to you."

It worked just like I knew it would. I was, after all, the get-rid-of-Miranda expert. She never spent another night in my room.

"Listen to your fans and understand you can get even better with constructive criticism. After all, beauty gurus share to help everyone." —**Torrey Grey, Beautystarz15**

CHAPTER THREE

GO TO CLASS WITH A TOTALLY TRENDY BACKPACK

Raylene turns off the car and I get my first look at Huntsville High School. Massive square brick columns frame the entrance to the building. The bike racks on either side of the wide front sidewalk are half full and the concrete steps leading up to the glass front doors are crowded with kids laughing and jostling for position.

"Are you scared?" Raylene asks me.

"Of what?" My mind is still on the moonstone bracelet. On the monsters that used to haunt my sister's bedroom.

"New school. New friends. I would be."

"I'm not you," I say, which is obvious.

For just a moment I feel bad, like I'm being too mean, but Raylene doesn't even seem to notice. I feel buzzy and light-headed. Walking into that school is the last thing I want to do.

Back in Colorado, school never made me nervous. Everyone knew who I was. Beautystarz15. If they were lucky, I might even tag one of them in a best-friend vlog, but the competition for that was fierce.

Now I don't know how to be the new kid.

The new kid with a past.

"Then I'll just be scared for you," Raylene says. After the brief moment of silence, she reaches across me to tug open the glove compartment and fumbles around inside. "I need a Snickers."

She comes up with a trick-or-treat-sized bar, which she unwraps quickly and pops into her mouth. Silently, she chews for a minute, with one hand held out dramatically to hold the conversation — except I'm not saying anything. Finally, she swallows.

"Okay. I'm ready."

"Great," I say under my breath. Searching through my purse for lip gloss, I try to ignore the fact that my hands are shaking a bit when I apply it. Raylene gets out, slamming the door behind her, and waits by the front fender.

You can do this.

Lights. Camera. Action. Showtime.

I'm grateful for my usual shield of hair products and lipstick as I get out of the car. Then I follow Raylene's cowboy boots toward the building.

There are plenty of curious stares when we walk by, but I can't tell if anyone actually recognizes me or not. It's weird. When I look around at all these new faces, I can't separate the computer world from the real world anymore. Everyone is a stranger now.

Or not.

Does the short-haired girl with the cat eyeliner standing

over by the water fountain KNOW me? Does she know I wash my face with Neutrogena Fresh Foaming Cleanser every night before bed? What about her giggling friend with the volleyball under one arm? Has she seen the ruffled pink pillows on my bed? Or the girls texting over by the lockers: Did they retweet that link about my favorite deals and steals in July?

Do they know about Miranda?

I realize it's just a matter of time before everyone at my new school knows, and then it will be like it was before I left Colorado. Once it is out in the open, they will avoid my eyes and say things like *so sorry* or *thinking of you*. If they say anything at all. Awkward. Embarrassing. Tragic.

But at least then I will know where I stand.

Raylene shows me the administrative office and gives me another one of her big hugs before leaving me on my own.

I spend a long half hour with a lot of blahblahblah from a worried school counselor who looks a lot like Abraham Lincoln and keeps tapping his fingers on his desk.

"I talked to your dad last week on the phone and he told me that you've been going through a tough time. I'm sorry to hear about your sister."

"Thank you." I now know that's what you are supposed to say.

"Your dad also said there was some negative publicity. I want you to know we don't tolerate cyberbullying of any kind here. Just tell me who's bothering you and we'll put a quick stop to it." He stops tapping his fingers, places both hands flat on the desktop, and leans across the desk toward me.

I blink at him. He thinks he can keep thousands of people from all over the world from posting comments about me? Obviously, he's clueless about the scope here. "Thanks," I say again.

"Now, you're going to have to catch up a bit on your schoolwork, Victoria." He clears his throat.

"My name isn't Victoria. It's Torrey," I say.

He wrinkles his forehead, trying to make the connection.

I spell out my name for him, letter by letter. "Torreys Peak is a fourteener in Colorado," I explain. "A mountain that's at least fourteen thousand feet high?"

He still looks oblivious.

"My parents climbed Torreys before I was born. My dad proposed to my mom on the summit, so they thought it'd be cool to name their first child in honor of that day."

He doesn't care.

"Never mind," I say. Mountains. Summits. Fourteeners. It's like talking in a different language in this flat, hot place.

"Okay, so let's get you to class," he says. He squints over the top of his reading glasses at his computer screen and types in something. Over his shoulder, the blinds of his office window are open, with a view of the crowded hallway. I watch the steady stream of kids walking past. Nobody is dressed to my standards. No big surprise.

"I know this is difficult, but we all want" — the counselor clasps his long fingers together — "to help you fit in here."

I'm not sure I want to fit in. But I don't really want to stand out, either.

After some concluding "blahblahblahblahblahblah . . . besureandaskifyouneedhelp . . . blahblah," the counselor issues me a stack of textbooks and finally lets me out of his office.

My English class is at the end of a long hallway. I'm hoping all the noise coming from behind the door means the teacher hasn't started yet. Taking one long breath of air, in through my nose and out through my mouth, I raise my chin and turn the knob.

The first thing I see is a wildly waving Raylene in the front row.

"I didn't know you were in this class! Sit with me," she calls out.

I flinch and glance around quickly to see who's watching, but everyone seems more concerned with getting into a chair before the bell rings. Thankfully, all the vacant chairs around Raylene are quickly occupied.

"Sorry," I tell her with a shrug.

I slide the "New Admit" sheet across the teacher's desk, not really looking at the woman behind it, and head toward an empty desk near the back wall. There are a couple of curious glances my way, but no outright stares. Not like it was every day of my last two weeks in Colorado. No shoulder punches, either. Or pointing. Or whispering behind hands.

Or videotaping with phones hidden under desktops. None that I can see anyway.

I take a seat. Across the aisle from me is a greasy-haired boy with an open copy of *Lord of the Flies* in front of him. I give him a quick nod. One side of his mouth goes up slightly, and I take that to be a smile, but he doesn't actually look at me. The guy next to him on the other side, however, is looking directly at me. He's hard to miss, with muscular arms that stretch out the short sleeves of his plain blue T-shirt, and dark brown eyes that are openly checking me out. Great hair, perfectly black and perfectly straight. He doesn't smile.

"Good morning, class," the teacher calls out cheerfully. Her voice sounds like Minnie Mouse. She's round and thirty-ish, with thick dark bangs. "Looks like the morning pep rally has us all running a little late on the schedule. Let's see who all we have here today."

When I look back at the brown-eyed boy, he is no longer staring at me.

The teacher starts the roll call.

"Ross Adams?"

A blond boy wearing a red plaid shirt answers. "Here."

I study him briefly. He has a tall, lanky build that reminds me a bit of my boyfriend, Cody. *Ex-boyfriend,* I remind myself.

"Raylene Anderson?"

Raylene waves with a jangle of silver bracelets. "Here."

"Blair Cunningham?"

Silence.

"Blair?" The teacher slides her pink-flowered reading glasses off her nose and scans the room. She puts them back on and makes a mark on the paper in front of her.

As she works her way down the alphabet, getting closer to the *Gs*, I tense up. I wonder how she'll introduce me and if there will be any obvious name recognition. My stomach clinches in anticipation.

"Torrey Grey?"

"Here," I say quickly. I sit up taller. Here it comes. The teacher is going to say something to the class about me.

But before even a single head can turn my direction, there's a stir at the door and three giggling girls enter. Everything pauses. Even the teacher stops to look and I'm released from the impending glare of the spotlight.

The girl in the center is obviously the princess, and she's wearing a Cavalli print dress that must have cost at least five hundred dollars. It's clear the other two are mere attendants to her highness. One of them, a tiny girl with a blond braid down her back, is wearing a cheerleading outfit with a big green hornet on her chest. The other one is a tall redhead with a permanent-looking sneer on her face. Both perfectly complement the dark-haired, dark-skinned girl in the expensive dress. I narrow my eyes and focus in on the object of everyone's attention, feeling the envy crawl up into my head. In another world, I was her.

And you can be again.

"We have excuses from the counselor, Mrs. Vardeman. Promise." The princess is at least a size twelve, with a voice just as big. She projects like she's speaking from a stage, and the audience responds with a perfectly timed round of appreciative laughter.

"Take your seat, Miss Cunningham," the teacher says.

The girls descend on three empty chairs in the row beside me and instantly, as if a wand is waved over the class, everything goes back to the way it was before their entry. In spite of myself, I'm impressed.

The teacher continues to call out names and I try to relax.

"Luis Rivera?"

"Here." It's the dark-eyed boy across the room. The princess, Blair, gives a disgusted groan and rolls her eyes.

Why?

"Mia Rogers?"

The blond cheerleader stops whispering to her friends long enough to quickly answer. The redheaded girl with the curls to die for responds to the name "Emily Sanderson."

I notice that the dark-haired girl, Blair, is watching me. I flip my braid back over my shoulder, trying to look confident. It's the first rule of being in front of the camera. Never appear nervous.

"You're new," she says, looking me up and down. She doesn't even whisper.

I stare back at her. It isn't a question, so it doesn't deserve an answer. But I smile.

Trust your instincts. You know how to do this.

"I like your jacket," she says. She faces me. Turned sideways in the desk and leaning forward across the aisle, she ignores the talking teacher at the front of the room.

"Thanks," I say.

"Abercrombie?"

"Yes."

"You look" — her eyes narrow at me — "familiar."

My head is humming. I wait.

"Blair, class has started," the teacher calls out. "I need your attention."

Blair grants it graciously, sliding her body around in the chair to face the front of the room, but not before a final comment to me. "You're going to burn up in that wool."

"Sorry," she says loudly to the teacher, and her two friends giggle like it's a huge joke.

Mrs. Vardeman finishes calling roll and steps to the center of the room. "Today we are discussing our third English Romantic poet, John Keats. Mr. Rivera, can you tell us the names of the other two poets we discussed?"

Luis, the dark-haired boy who stared at me, answers quickly. "Byron and Shelley."

"Correct."

"Freak," Blair whispers under her breath. She's staring intently across the room.

I look back at the boy. Tall. Wide shoulders. He doesn't look like an outcast from society, but Blair's message is clear. *Stay away from him. He's not one of us.*

"Frankenstein has all the answers today," Mia the cheerleader mumbles; and Emily the redhead snickers.

Blair looks at me and arches her eyebrows like she's asking me to agree. I nod back at her like I completely understand, but I don't.

The teacher is talking on and on. Something about romance and rhyme and themes. I can't really focus on anything she says. Instead, I spend the rest of class wondering how to make this whole new-school thing work. My father and I have always been alike in this way. We both need to fix things.

Just as the bell rings, memory invades again.

Miranda's obsession with superheroes went viral when she was about ten. She watched them on TV, read about them, drew them, and even dressed like them. I was fourteen, and found it totally baffling.

"Guess who this is," she said. She was talking while she was drawing in her sketchbook. We were sitting at FroYo's waiting for Mom to finish grocery shopping and I was annoyed I forgot my earbuds.

"Batman," I said, not looking.

"Not even close. Guess again."

I was flipping through a new copy of Seventeen *magazine, getting impatient with her little game.*

"It kind of looks like Superman," I said, glancing over at her sketch pad, "but it's a girl, right?"

"Yes . . ." she said eagerly.

"So . . . SuperGIRL?" I asked. I went back to my magazine. I was just starting to become fascinated with fashion and beauty.

"Nope," Miranda said, sucking in her lips like she was holding on to the biggest secret ever.

"I give up." I wasn't really trying that hard at guessing and we both knew it.

"Ta-da!" She made jazz hands beside her face. "It's YOU."

"Me?"

She stretched the words out into each individual syllable. "Sen . . . sa . . . tion . . . al Sis . . . ter."

I looked a little closer at the picture, seeing for the first time the long brown hair and the blue eyes. I laughed. "What's my superpower?"

"You fix things. Like hair and makeup and clothes."

I was flattered. "A lot of people do that," I said, even though among my friends I was becoming the known expert on where to find the right lip gloss. "It isn't exactly a special power."

"Well . . ." She colored in the cape with her red drawing pencil while she thought. "You also fix other things."

"Like?"

"Remember when I was afraid of the dark and you gave me that bracelet?"

"The moonstone?" I hadn't thought of it in years. "That was a long time ago."

"It worked." She colored in a blue circle around the wrist of the smaller figure on the page while I watched. "You fixed it."

There was a tightness in my throat.

"And this is me." Miranda pointed at the smaller girl in the picture. The prickles in my throat grew stronger, the magazine in front of me forgotten, while she busily added in the yellow curls all around the smiling face.

"Can I have it?" I asked.

"What for?" She looked up from her drawing, her blond hair in her face.

"Because I like being Sensational Sister." I reached over and pushed one wild curl away from her forehead.

She looked at me like she didn't believe me, but wanted to.

"Sure," she said, and handed it over.

"Keep up to date on trends and events. It's all about fostering a stronger connection with your future viewers."

—Torrey Grey, Beautystarz15

CHAPTER FOUR

SAY GOOD-BYE TO SUMMER WITH MIRRORED SUNGLASSES

Two hours and one incomprehensible biology class later, it's lunchtime.

Blair and Raylene were right: I got hot in my woolen blazer, so I stowed it in my new locker on my way to the cafeteria. Now I stand in my jeans and T-shirt, feeling queasy and scanning the crowded cafeteria. I'm determined to find the most inconspicuous place possible to sit. The peanut-butter-and-grape-jelly sandwich I slapped together this morning will buy me a quick ticket to a table in a far, ordinary corner and give me the perfect viewing spot to assess the haves and the have-nots.

I start walking as though I know where I'm going. I don't, but hesitation will just draw attention from the chatting, laughing tables. People will glance up, then they'll start tapping friends on shoulders and whispering.

Did you see that article in Teen Vogue?

I saw her on the Ten YouTube Beauty Gurus to Watch.

Did you hear about her sister?

There are a few completely empty tables way back on the right, but I don't want to sit all by myself. That's bound to draw the attention of some perky do-gooder with a mission to welcome newcomers to the high school. Not happening. So, I keep walking, scanning for a not-too-empty bench.

I spot Blair, Mia, and Emily over at a table by the windows, obviously a prime location. I hear Blair, the princess, shriek with laughter, but I don't look in her direction long.

It's clear Huntsville High School is like any other high school. There are three main groups. The popular group, the semipopular group, and the want-to-be popular group. Some people might claim there is a fourth group of Goths and all the self-styled freaks who don't care about high school high society, but I lump them in with the want-to-bes. I mean, black lipstick and all that eyeliner? It's about attention, and that's really what being popular is anyway, right?

At my old school, I was lucky enough to be in the popular group even before the vlog hit it big. What most people don't know is that popularity isn't just about location in the cafeteria. Back in Colorado, my friends and I did an experiment one week where we changed tables every single day. It didn't matter. We still sat by the same exact people because everyone followed us wherever we moved. One day by the windows. The next by the trash cans. Day after day, for the whole week. The semipopulars and the want-to-bes were completely confused and wandered around aimlessly looking for new seats.

It was hysterical.

"It's a lot of work being in such demand," Zoe said after the third time we found somewhere new to sit. "But I guess if it was super easy to be popular, then it wouldn't be so special."

Am I too much work now, Zoe?

I come to a table that's occupied just by a blond guy wearing a black T-shirt with a pi symbol on the front. He's cute, in a geeky-cool kind of way. I figure I won't find another table at this point, so I set down my lunch bag.

He glances up from the iPad in front of him and I give him a quick nod. His eyes are a bit unfocused and his attention immediately goes back to the screen. I pull out my apple, plastic bottle of orange juice, and the sandwich, arranging them to look like I am eating lunch normally. But nothing about this feels normal. I belong at the table with Blair and her friends.

A curvy brown-haired girl slides onto the bench next to the blond boy. She has earbuds in and her head bobs in time to the music. I don't recognize either the girl or the guy from my morning classes, so I think they might be older.

The girl meets my gaze and pulls out her earbuds.

"Hi, I'm Ever," she says, and smiles. She has the most gorgeous green eyes.

"Ever?" I repeat the unusual name.

"Yeah. Like the fairy tale. Happily Ever After." She smiles again, as if she's laughing at herself. There's something about her that I like. But she *is* sitting at a half-empty table. Not a good sign for her social status. "What's your name?" she asks me.

"Torrey Grey," I answer reluctantly.

"Like the color?"

I nod. I don't see any recognition in her eyes. Not surprising, since she seems to be into a natural, low-key kind of look. Beauty vlogs are probably not her thing. She's still pretty though.

Before she can say anything else, the boy beside her looks up again and starts talking. "It says right here the ancient Aztecs believed that monarch butterflies were the souls of their fallen warriors and should be honored."

"Fascinating," Ever says to him, "but I'm not convinced."

I uncap my juice bottle, and the boy looks over at me. "I want to track the migration of monarch butterflies to Mexico," he explains earnestly, as if I've asked. "It's really all about tagging. I'd have to associate the location of capture with the point of recovery for each butterfly."

Ever rolls her eyes, then gives me an apologetic grin. "Will you stop?" she tells the boy. "All I'm saying is it won't hurt you to take an elective other than science."

"I like science." He scowls.

"You should try something new. Maybe an art class? Expand your horizons."

"Tagging monarchs is new," he says, but with less certainty this time.

Ever gives him a green-eyed glare. A sudden grin transforms his face and he reaches out to take her hand. Slowly his fingers intertwine with hers and her mouth twitches up in a half smile.

"Maybe I can learn how to draw a monarch butterfly," he says.

"I'd like that," she says softly.

I glance away quickly, feeling a sudden pang. The intimacy makes me uncomfortable. Cody was cute and fit in great with my friends — but I know I never looked at him that way. And he never looked that way at me, either.

How does he look at Zoe?

I pull my phone out of my bag. Still no text from my supposed best friend.

"Hey," I hear the boy across the table say. I glance up from my phone. "I'm Rat," he says, as if he's just realized there's another person at the table and he needs to introduce himself.

Rat? I hope it's a nickname and Texans don't name their children after rodents.

Suddenly, Rat looks down at his watch. "Don't you have a rehearsal?" he asks Ever.

"Right." She shakes her head and reaches for his arm, sliding her hand down to his wrist to check out the watch for herself.

"I should go. I'm late." Her hand lingers.

"I'll walk you," Rat says. When he grins, he doesn't look geeky at all. He just looks adorable.

Ever stands to leave, gathering up her things quickly. "Nice meeting you," she says to me, and Rat waves a quick good-bye. I watch as they walk off together, hand in hand.

I sit alone, sort of missing the presence of Ever and Rat, even though they're not the kind of people I'd want to really befriend.

I stare at the uneaten sandwich in front of me. I was lucky to find something that resembles a lunch. Grocery shopping hasn't exactly been a high priority in our house these days. Dad's new job keeps him late, and Mom spends all her time in our new vegetable garden.

The noise of the crowded cafeteria blurs into a dull roar. My eyelids are so heavy. A body can only go so long without sleep before it shuts down. If I could put my head down on the table and close my eyes without drawing attention to myself, I would.

"You're Torrey, right?"

My eyes startle open. I knock the apple off the table and it rolls across the floor toward the boy standing in front of me.

It's Luis. The dark-eyed boy from my English class. I don't answer, but he squeezes into the bench across from me, slipping his backpack off his shoulders.

He picks up the apple off the floor and hands it back to me without a word. I carefully place it back on the table. My palms are damp with sweat and I wipe them off on my jeans.

"Yeah," I say, trying to act as if I wasn't just half asleep.

"I'm Luis. I'm in your English class?" He waits like I'm supposed to say something back.

I shrug my shoulders.

So? And you're evidently a freak. You just don't look like one.

I glance around quickly and my stomach sinks when I spot Mia staring at us. She taps Blair on the shoulder and motions in our direction. Then they both stare. The message is clear from the daggers being flung our way: If I ever want the slightest chance to move up to their table, I need to get rid of this guy.

"What do you want?" I ask him curtly.

His forehead creases into a frown.

"I was just going to tell you that I'm sorry about your sister." Luis's voice is low and steady.

Suddenly everything freezes.

"How do you know about that?" I catch the sharpness in my voice.

"My dad owns the funeral home in town. It's a family business."

Is that why he's unpopular? Because he works in the funeral home? That could explain why kids would make fun of him.

"I met your mom and dad at your sister's graveside ceremony," Luis goes on as I sit, unmoving. "They said you'd be coming to school here." He looks right at me when he says it, not like all my friends in Boulder, who never quite met my eyes after they heard about Miranda. I look back at his dark eyes. I feel the heat creeping up my neck, the realization of what he's saying sinking in slowly. He was there watching my sister being put in the ground.

This isn't about a boy hitting on the new girl in school. This isn't about my vlog. It's about pity — and I don't need that from anyone.

I feel tears welling up behind my eyelids. The weakness just makes me angry, and I blink the emotion quickly away. He's not going to get a reaction from me.

"I like eating lunch alone," I tell him pointedly, picking up my sandwich.

He blinks. "I just wanted to say hello."

"Yeah, thanks." I take a bite of my sandwich and stare back down at the cafeteria table.

Out of the corner of my eye, I see him gather up his lunch and backpack and start to walk away. I wait, my heart ticking away in my chest.

Did he tell anyone else?

When I look up again, there's no sign of Luis, and I catch Blair watching me with a half smile of approval. I know there's no way she heard our exchange, but at least she saw me get rid of him. That's what counts. Right?

SensorOnline

DRUNK DRIVER PLEADS GUILTY IN DEATH OF GIRL

Published on: September 15, 6:28:13 PM MDT

Boulder, Colorado — The man accused in a deadly DUI case was back in court this morning. Steve Waters, 53, has been charged with felony drunken driving and vehicular manslaughter in the death of a 12-year-old Boulder girl. Waters was driving on 10th Street near the Pearl Street Mall when he hit and killed Miranda Grey. Grey was in the crosswalk at the time. Court records show Waters's blood alcohol level was more than twice the legal limit.

Judge Patricia Jules accepted Steve Waters's withdrawal of a not guilty plea to manslaughter. Waters then pleaded guilty. Judge Jules scheduled Waters's sentencing hearing for December 15. The sentencing is expected to last two days while attorneys present evidence. Prosecuting attorney Margaret Richardson says she expects a representative from the Grey family to present a victim impact statement.

"Keep on shopping." —**Torrey Grey, Beautystarz15**

CHAPTER FIVE

GET GLAM AND GIRLY WITH FALL'S BEST LOOKS

I hate coming home. Not that I can call this flat, unremarkable house a home. The walls are all beige and the cheap furniture looks like it was paid off in monthly payments over a very long period of time. There's one picture of a field of blue flowers over the brown faux leather couch in the living room, and that's all.

None of the familiar stuff from our old house in Boulder is here. None of *her* familiar stuff. There are no dirty tennis shoes to trip over and no art supplies to move off the table every time we eat. Everything of Miranda's, including the paints and the shoes, are packed away in unlabeled boxes and stacked in the corner of the dirty two-car garage. But even in a new house in a new town, there is no boxing up Miranda. She is everywhere. And nowhere.

I find my mom in the kitchen.

"How was your first day at school?" She is carefully lining up her newly washed tomatoes on a dish towel. She doesn't look up, but she actually asked me a question, so I guess that's progress.

She also doesn't wait for an answer.

"Look at these. The growing season lasts so long here." She's actually smiling. Not at me, but at the tomatoes. "It's too bad you don't like tomatoes. You wouldn't believe the difference between store-bought and these from that tangle of a garden somebody left behind."

Miranda is the one who didn't like tomatoes. She doesn't remember.

I grab some cereal out of the pantry. As I pull open the fridge for the milk, Mom finally glances up from the tomatoes.

"I can't believe how many mosquitoes are out there. Colorado had mosquitoes, if it wasn't too cold. But here, they gather in doorways in big black clouds and just wait for you."

"I noticed," I say, and then ask, "Is Dad still at work?"

She blinks, the question registering slowly, and I realize she has no idea. She mumbles, "I think he said he was going to be late tonight."

Moving as if in slow motion, she washes off two more tomatoes in the sink and then asks, "Did you take the bus home?"

One time, when she was in the fourth grade, Miranda missed the school bus home. She was sitting at the stop with the bus in front of her, but she was so totally involved in her library book, she didn't even get on it. The bus took off without her and she had to call Dad to come pick her up. My dad was furious he had to leave work, but later it became this big joke in the family.

"No," I say, "Raylene drove me."

I sit down at the table and pour the Rice Krispies into my bowl. "Do you want some?" I ask Mom. "You really should eat." This is backward. It should be the mom reminding the kid to eat.

"I'm not hungry," Mom says, but she does turn around and join me at the table. She sits still, fiddling with a spoon in front of her.

She seems so far away. I want to tell her I miss her and that I don't want to be alone anymore, but I can't push those words out past the big lump in my throat.

I pour the milk on my cereal and take a big bite. When I speak again, I try to keep my voice casual. "Dad and I were talking about me getting my driver's license. All my driving hours will transfer from Colorado. I checked. All I have to do is take the test. I think it's probably a good idea, right?" I say it all really fast and then stuff another spoonful of cereal into my mouth.

Mom's forehead creases into long lines. She leans forward and her blond curls, so like Miranda's, fall into her face. "Are you old enough?" she asks.

"I'm sixteen, Mom."

"That's right." She smiles ever so slightly.

I focus all my attention on stirring the cereal into a mushy mess and then watch it spin wildly around in the milk funnel

I created. Some milk splashes onto the table and Mom reaches over as if she's going to wipe it up, or take my hand to stop me from stirring. It's like her mom instincts kick in for one second. But one second only. She pulls her hand back and drops it listlessly into her lap.

"I'm not so sure about you driving," she says. "It's dangerous."

We both know what she's talking about. "I'll be careful," I say.

"Do you have any homework?" she asks quietly, changing the subject.

I look up from the bowl into her pale blue eyes.

"Just some biology reading," I answer, even though I can tell she isn't listening.

The driver's license subject is obviously not going anywhere. I decide to tackle the next big subject. There is little hope it's going to go any better, but I have to try.

"I've been thinking about the court thing."

My mom freezes, her back stiffening. This is definitely going to be worse.

"What court thing?" she asks, each word an effort to produce.

"The district attorney said someone from the family will be able to give a statement in court. I want to be the one to do it."

She sort of cough-chokes. "What brought this up, Torrey?"

I shrug, as if I haven't been thinking about it since Raylene mentioned it this morning. "I'm good at talking in front of people. It's my . . . our . . . opportunity to tell our side of the story," I say slowly, determined to keep going.

Mom stands up suddenly with the spoon in her hand. Her back is rigid, unyielding, as she puts the spoon down on the countertop with an abrupt clatter.

"This can wait. We don't have to talk about it right now," she says sharply.

"You can't even say what *this* is." My voice rises.

Mom turns toward me, her eyes glittering with raw pain, no longer unfocused and vague. "Miranda is dead and we're supposed to tell everyone how that makes us *feel*? What good is it going to do?" she demands bitterly.

I realize I have pierced her stupor of grief. But there is no victory in seeing what lies beneath.

Without a word, Mom stalks out of the kitchen. In a minute, I hear her bedroom door slam. The guilt of my accomplishment hits like a hammer to my stomach. The plain beige walls of the kitchen close in on me.

I leave the rest of the cereal on the table and go to my own room. I throw myself on my bed and stare up at the ceiling. I feel like I am supposed to cry, but I'm not sad. I'm mad. I want my used-to-be life back.

After a minute, I sit up and unzip my backpack. May as well get started on that biology homework. A single piece of folded paper slides out of the backpack and falls to the floor. I pick it up, open it, and read the message scrawled there.

Go home, Beautystarz15.

It takes a minute for the words to sink in. Somebody recognized me today.

My stomach squeezes. Who was it? I think through the day, tightening and loosening the shot on each new remembered face. Ross, the blond boy with the big smile who reminded me of Cody? Probably not. He doesn't seem like the type who'd know about beauty and fashion videos. Same goes for Ever and Rat, my lunch companions.

What about Princess Blair? She'd said I looked familiar. But the note slipped into a backpack doesn't seem like her style.

Then I remember. Luis. The funeral home boy. He knows about my sister. He probably Googled me or something and made the connection to my vlog. It has to be him.

I stare at the note in my hand. Is this supposed to be a threat? He thinks he knows all about me, but he obviously doesn't know who he's dealing with. Anger pours into my hands, making the slip of paper shake. I'm not about to be bullied by some high school freak.

I pull out my phone and type in the name of the funeral home. There is only one tiny bar of service and it takes forever, but finally it pops up on the screen. Luis Rivera's house, and his family business, is a quick bike ride away.

The heat is so intense that my T-shirt is plastered to my back by the time I've pedaled the few blocks. My energy and my anger have dwindled significantly with the effort.

I spot the big white sign that reads RIVERA FUNERAL HOME: FAMILY OWNED SINCE 1954. Directly next door is a big yellow house with a large front porch. I stop the bike and put one foot down on the sidewalk.

Two older women sit on wooden rocking chairs under a wildly spinning ceiling fan. One is a tall woman with tight gray curls who looks a little like my grandmother back in Colorado. The other is a tiny Hispanic woman wearing a bright pink beret covered in rhinestones.

I call out. "I'm looking for Luis Rivera. Does he live here?"

The gray-haired woman shouts back, "He's gone running. That boy doesn't have a lick of sense some days." She waves me up toward the porch. "Oh, Lord, it's hot out here today. Can't believe this September weather. You want some ice tea, honey?"

I wipe my sweaty forehead with the sleeve of my Lucky Brand T-shirt. It's too tempting to turn down.

"Yes, thank you," I say. I lay the bike down on the grass and join them.

"Sit right there on the swing. You're going to burn up in this sun." The gray-haired woman pours me a glass of tea from an icy pitcher on the plant stand nearby. I sit down on the swing and touch the icy glass to my forehead before taking a long drink.

"My name is Mrs. Annie Florence and this is Maria Rivera. She's Luis's *abuelita*. That means grandmother."

I know that because I took Spanish in Colorado for my foreign language elective, but I don't enlighten her. I just say, "Hello. I'm Torrey."

Mrs. Annie Florence nods and gives me a big grin. In spite of my reservations, I smile back. I can't seem to help it.

"Me and Maria have been best friends since we were kids. Now we're both widows and we're back together again," Mrs. Annie Florence tells me.

Maria speaks up for the first time, peering at me curiously. "I haven't seen you before. Do you go to school with Luis?" she asks.

"I'm new," I say, and take another big swig of the tea. The cool, sweet taste fills my throat and I feel myself relax. There is no sign of judgment here with these women.

"Luis will be back soon," Maria says. "You just cool off a bit and drink that ice tea."

"Isn't it cooler in the house?" I ask, hearing the rattle of the central air compressor behind me.

"You can't see anything in there," Maria explains. "We're waiting to catch sight of who all's coming to Mr. Paulson's viewing. I hear he left three different girlfriends and they've all been to the funeral parlor to pick out different things for him to wear into eternity."

Mrs. Annie Florence nods, then says, "Mr. Paulson had a zonkey ranch out on the east side of town."

"What kind of ranch?" I must have misunderstood her.

"Zonkeys," she says again. "He bought this zebra at a sale up near Cleveland, brought it back, and bred it with a donkey. Got zonkeys."

They must be kidding me. "Is that a real thing?" I ask Maria.

"Sí," she says, picking up the pitcher. *"¿Más?"*

I hold out my glass and she fills it back up to the top. I wonder what a zonkey looks like, but I'm suddenly distracted from that thought. I catch sight of something on the porch.

The pots of bright red geraniums almost hid them from view, but now I can clearly see the figurines everywhere. Figurines of skeletons.

A skeleton riding a bike. A skeleton playing a guitar. A skeleton in a wedding dress. I blink, startled by the figures on every corner, railing, and windowsill. My stomach tightens and I take a gulp of ice tea to calm the creepiness, but not before Maria notices.

"Do you like my *calacas*?" she asks.

"The skeletons? Yeah, sure. Happy Halloween." I raise my glass as a toast.

"It's not for Halloween," Mrs. Annie Florence says. "It's for *el Día de los Muertos*."

I translate the phrase in my head. *Day of the Dead*. The breeze from the rattling ceiling fan shakes the skeleton on the bike just enough to make it seem as if he's waving at me.

Oh yeah, that's better.

"It is not like Halloween at all," Maria says. "The whole point of *el Día de los Muertos* is to learn to live with death . . . make fun of it a little . . . and it won't hold so much power. That's why the skeletons look a little silly."

I glance around at the skeleton figures once more, but the grins on their little bony faces don't make me feel any better.

Maria sighs and clasps her hands to her chest. The glittery hat perched on her head wiggles with the motion. "*El Día de los Muertos* has been my favorite holiday ever since I was a child in Janitzio, Mexico," she says, then leans forward in her rocking chair and continues in a hushed voice. "Thousands of people came to our tiny town every year to celebrate. People spent all night beside the graves of their relatives, leaving *ofrendas* and building altars. The bell at the entrance to the cemetery chimed all night and, at midnight, the living and dead were thought to come back together again for that one special night."

Goose bumps go down my arms and I try to rub them away.

"Amazing," Mrs. Annie Florence breathes. "Someday I'm going to see that."

"Yeah, sounds great," I say, but I still avoid looking at the skeletons.

Maybe Mrs. Annie Florence sees something in my face, because she switches the subject. "Did you go to the Cortez viewing last week?" she asks Maria.

"Yes." Maria nods and rocks.

"How did she look?"

I'm thinking she must have looked dead.

I'm glad to be off the subject of the grinning skeletons and spending the night in graveyards, but quickly realize this isn't much better. I feel a trickle of sweat on my forehead begin to roll down the side of my cheek.

"Not natural," Maria says. "That new girl just doesn't have the gift."

"That's exactly what I told John!" Mrs. Annie Florence slaps the arm of her wooden rocking chair for emphasis.

"The corpses just haven't looked the same since Mrs. Annie Florence retired from the restorative arts business last February," Maria says to me.

"I always like to think of it as their last big makeover for eternity." Mrs. Annie smiles gently at me.

Who talks about these things? I nod as though this conversation is the most normal thing in the world, but start trying to come up with a good excuse to leave. Coming here was a mistake. I can talk to Luis at school.

"What are you doing here?"

It's too late. A shirtless Luis is standing in front of us on the sidewalk.

He swipes a crumpled red T-shirt across the smooth, caramel-colored skin of his chest, scowling in my direction. I was so distracted by the crazy talk on the porch, I didn't even hear him come up.

"Don't be rude, *nieto,*" Maria says. "Your friend here rode her bike all the way over in this heat to see you."

"My friend?" Luis echoes, looking over at me with raised eyebrows.

"I, um, I wanted to talk to you," I say, trying to sound resolved.

"Lo siento, Abuelita." Luis walks up the steps and greets both women with a quick kiss to the cheek. "I didn't mean to be impolite." Then he turns to me, his expression closing off. "I need to finish my workout," he tells me.

I'm not surprised. Nobody gets those kinds of abs from the gene pool. Luis turns and starts toward the building next door, glancing back over his shoulder. "You coming?" he asks.

I scramble off the porch, quickly saying my good-byes to the ladies and the grinning skeletons.

"If you want to talk to me, then you're going to have to do it while I'm working out. I don't have a lot of time. I'm on the night shift," Luis says.

"Doing what?" I'm almost scared to ask.

"Mr. Paulson's viewing. Evidently there's going to be some excitement."

"I heard," I say.

He walks so fast I can barely keep up, and unfortunately heads straight toward the funeral home, passing a black hearse parked in the back circle drive. Is his workout partner the corpse of a zonkey dealer? What, or who, else is inside? More skeletons? I really don't want to find out.

Luis glances back to notice I've slowed down. One side of his mouth crooks into a smile. "Don't worry. We're going downstairs."

Like that's supposed to make me feel better?

"Beauty is deeper than makeup. It's an art form."

—Torrey Grey, Beautystarz15

CHAPTER SIX
FLIRTING TRICKS THAT WORK

I slowly follow Luis to an unmarked door. He bends down and pulls up the corner of a mat on the step, revealing a key. He unlocks the door and holds it open for me. I freeze on the step, but the grin on his face is a test I'm not about to fail.

"We're going down the stairs," he says again, and flips on the light switch.

"What's upstairs?" I ask.

"A formaldehyde prep room, three embalming tables, six dressing tables, a cooler processing station." He pauses for a beat. "And Mr. Paulson."

"Well, then I'm definitely going downstairs." I slide past him and down the steps. I hear him following behind.

The large unfinished basement is like a mini gym. A long metal bar and a set of rings hang from the ceiling. The floor is covered with mats, and a set of free weights lines the wall next to a punching bag. No caskets. No bodies. I start to breathe a little easier.

"You must spend a lot of time down here," I say.

"I've seen lots of dead bodies. But this . . ." He holds out one arm and slowly clinches his hand into a fist. I see the movement of the muscle under his skin. "This makes me feel alive," he says. "The body is an amazing machine. I don't want to ever take it for granted."

He jumps for the bar above his head and does a slow pull-up. "So are you going to tell me what this is about?" he asks.

Every vein in his forearms shows with the effort. But there is no sign of effort in his expression. He does three more pull-ups while I watch. I realize my mouth is hanging open and I shut it with a snap. *What's wrong with me?* The note, I remind myself. That's why I'm here. I pull the note out of my jeans pocket and unfold it.

"Why did you write this?" I hold it out toward him.

"What is it?" He drops down from the bar in one fluid motion and walks over to me, picking up a couple of free weights from the rack on the way. He puts the weights on the floor beside my feet and then straightens, glancing down at the outstretched paper in my hand.

"Sorry. Wasn't me." He says it in such a matter-of-fact way, and his face is so serious, I suddenly have doubts. Maybe I jumped to conclusions.

I stand awkwardly in front of him, shifting from foot to foot. "You didn't write it?"

"Nope." He runs a hand through his dark hair and looks down at me. His eyes are so brown they are almost black. "Who is Beautystarz15?"

"Never mind," I say, and all my bravado rushes out in one deep breath. I feel really stupid. And suddenly stuck. It's not like I can just leave now. I rode over here on a bike and sat out on that porch with his grandmother and Mrs. Annie Florence, waiting for him. After all that trouble, how would it look if I left after only two minutes? I fumble for a reason for my visit and only come up with stupid small talk.

"Your grandmother is quite the collector. Skeletons? Kind of strange, don't you think?"

All that ad-libbing on camera comes in handy sometimes. I'm good at coming up with stuff on the fly, and it helps to include a little bit of the truth when you can. Makes everything more believable.

"It's not just the skeletons," Luis replies with a small smile. "She loves everything about *el Día de los Muertos*. The food, the *ofrendas*, the flowers. Everything." He drops the weight, picks up the other one with his left hand, and repeats the exercise. "It's her favorite holiday — even bigger than Christmas."

"I guess it makes sense with the family business and all." I grimace, then catch myself and flash him one of my winning smiles. He's not fooled.

"You didn't have to come here. We could have talked at school." He looks at me with raised eyebrows. "Especially if it makes you so uncomfortable."

But Blair thinks you're a freak and I don't want to be seen with you.

"Tell me about the whole *ofrenda* thing." I'm grasping at straws, buying time until I can come up with something better.

"First, pick up one of the weights," he says, his eyes still locked on mine.

"Why?"

"My answer will cost you ten push-ups."

"You can't be serious."

But he is.

"I don't want to be stared at," he says. "I work out. You work out."

Reluctantly, I drop down on my knees beside him. He's already in a perfect plank position and holding it. He glances sideways at me.

"Like this." Effortlessly, he lowers himself slowly to the ground and back up again.

I let my arms hold my weight and lower my body. I barely know how to do a push-up. Exercise was always more of Miranda's thing. She loved being outside in all the dirt and sweat. Me? Not so much. I've never lifted a weight in my life, and right now it's definitely showing. I'm lucky to have my dad's build — tall and naturally thin. I struggle through six more push-ups before I go down and stay down.

"What's an *ofrenda*?" I mumble into the mat.

"You didn't make it to ten," he says, still doing push-ups.

I drag myself up off the mat with a groan and sit back against the mirror, glaring at him. "Really?"

"Okay. Okay." He's grinning now and still doing push-ups. "During *el Día de los Muertos* families usually decorate the graves with *ofrendas*, or offerings. *Ofrendas* can be favorite foods or possessions. The idea is whatever made the dead happy in life, they are to have again."

Like a moonstone bracelet to keep away the nightmares? I push that thought down. I don't even know where that silly bracelet is now. What did make Miranda happy in life? Do I even know anymore? That's a big problem if I want to tell a courtroom full of people about the impact of her death. I stretch one arm out across my body to ease the tightness.

"So, for example, what would be a good *ofrenda* for you?" Luis asks.

I answer quickly without much thought, "My Marc Jacobs python tote."

He laughs at that. "So you get the idea."

He picks up a fifteen-pound weight off the rack and hands it to me. "Triceps curls with squats. I'll show you."

I glare at him in the mirror, but he ignores me, raising the thirty-pound weight up and down behind his back. The curve of the muscle under his shoulder moves and hardens. He glances over to see me watching.

"Feet shoulder-width apart. Now sit back like you're sitting down in a chair. Like this."

Reluctantly, I stand and pick up the weight in front of me.

"When you put stress on a muscle it can cause a tear — a rip. The body works to repair itself and makes the muscle even stronger."

I raise the weight up by my ear and back down again, feeling the underside of my arms burn.

He keeps talking, completely ignoring my struggle. "It's survival. The harder you work, the stronger a body gets. The heavier weight is interpreted as a threat. Pretty amazing, don't you think?"

"Great," I say. Now my arms and thighs are screaming in pain. This is way too much trouble. Sweaty has never been a good look for me. I squat down three more times, raising and lowering the weight behind my head. Finally, I give up, putting the weight on the floor in front of me, panting with the effort.

"How do you live surrounded by all this" — I point up toward the ceiling and whatever is upstairs — "creepy stuff?" It surprises me how suddenly very important his answer is. "I mean, do you just . . . get used to it?"

He doesn't pretend to not understand what I'm talking about. "It's normal for me. I did my homework at the kitchen table and my dad would work on rebuilding facial features on a blank Styrofoam head." Luis leans over, picks up the weight off the floor, and slowly lifts it up to his shoulder, flexing his bicep. "Sometimes, with advanced decomposition, that's a real challenge. He would tell me if my algebra equation was wrong and sometimes I'd tell him the ears were off. It wasn't strange. It was just how it was."

"Isn't that kind of morbid?" I ask.

"You're asking me?" He laughs. "My whole life is morbid."

I think about telling him I understand, in a way. That since Miranda died, death has become a part of our family, too. But I don't say anything.

"I have to get cleaned up," Luis says, putting the weights away. "Mrs. Haddock is always early." He picks up his T-shirt off the bench. "She's ninety-two and comes to every viewing. According to her, we have the best cookies. She likes to call all her friends who can't drive anymore and tell them what the body was wearing."

He pulls the shirt on over his head, leaving his hair a dark, spiky mess. "If you want to talk more, I'm at the track most mornings before school. We can run while we talk."

"Run?" I say, my head still swirling with talk of *ofrendas* and skeletons, weights and muscles, living and dying.

"You know how to run, right?" Luis says.

"I know how. I just don't do it unless someone's chasing me."

He grins widely. "Okay, then. I'll chase you."

BEAUTYBASHER.COM

**Board Index*FAQ*News*Chat*Register*Login*

Board Index/Trash a Beauty Vlogger/Beautystarz15
TORREY'S SISTER KILLED
Re: TORREY'S SISTER KILLED

Simplystylish wrote: That's honestly so awful. I wonder if she'll ever be back or if she won't be able to recover.

Re: Re: TORREY'S SISTER KILLED

Cheergirl wrote: If I were her, I'd put comments on approval. Some people are still talking about it on her videos.

Re: Re: Re: TORREY'S SISTER KILLED

QueenPink wrote: Has anyone else noticed she hasn't uploaded a video since it happened? I don't think she'll be back anytime soon.

Re: Re: Re: Re: TORREY'S SISTER KILLED

RUMad wrote: Comments are on approval now. If she really wants to return to YouTube, I'm sure she will. I would need time too if I was her.

Re: Re: Re: Re: Re: TORREY'S SISTER KILLED

LookNgood wrote: Her channel is back up. She hasn't made a new video yet, but I have a feeling she will soon. Wonder if she'll say anything about her sister.

"You're never alone on YouTube." —**Torrey Grey, Beautystarz15**

CHAPTER SEVEN

DREAMY COLOR COMBOS THAT WON'T WASH YOU OUT

That night, after I come back from Luis's house, I take a shower, change into a new outfit, and reapply my makeup. Then I set up to film a vlog in my bedroom.

The online gossipers are right. The pressure is building. If I don't post something soon, I'll start losing subscribers. Now is the time to talk about Miranda's death. It needs to be something simple — classic — just me talking to my subs and thanking them for all the support. Then everything can go back to normal.

I adjust the lighting by pulling over my bedside lamp, but I'm not thinking about beauty and fashion. Instead I'm thinking about Luis. I think about his grandmother and her friend talking about dead people like it's the most normal thing in the world. I think about his father re-creating noses at the kitchen table, but most of all I'm thinking about what Luis said about *ofrendas.*

Whatever made the dead happy in life, they are to have again.

How do you do that, exactly?

I check to make sure the shot is tight, just a close-up of my face without any sign of the boring beige-walled bedroom. I turn on the camera, sit down in the chair, and stare into the lens.

"Hello, Beauty Stars!" I give my signature wave and smile into the camera. "So I wanted to tell you all what I've been up to. . . ." My voice trails off. For some reason, the look of my fingers distracts me.

Sometimes I say I hate the way my fingers look. There's really nothing wrong with them, but you have to hate something about how you look, right? When other girls say, "Oh, I hate my hair. It's so curly," or another one says, "My thighs are huge," then I say, "I just hate my fingers. They are so stubby." I figure why not make the hated body part something that really doesn't count? Lately, though, I've been kind of thinking my fingers really are ugly. I stop the recording, watching my fingers carefully. I'll delete that clip. I push RECORD again.

"Hello, Beauty Stars!" *Do the wave again. Don't focus on your fingers.* "I'm so sorry I haven't posted for so long. So many of you have tweeted to ask where I've been lately and I wanted to update you. . . ."

I stop recording, then watch the clip. Even with the extra lamp, the lighting is horrible. And you can make out a sliver of the wall behind me. A hint of the bedroom.

The tour of my room back in Colorado was one of the most-viewed posts. There were countless comments on my pink walls, vintage pillows, and cute closet-organizing techniques. My subs will note the difference. How am I supposed to explain this? The face reflected in the monitor is like a ghost over the images on screen. My eyes look so tired. And sad. The tears well up and spill silently down my cheeks. It's all too much. I don't know where to start.

I wipe my tears off my face with the back of one hand. The mascara has smeared. This isn't what my fans sign on to watch. They want to see whether I'm wearing purple Toms or gray New Balance sneakers. They want me to tell them whether to buy a MAC 224 crease brush or a MAC 217 blending brush for their Bobbi Brown eye shadow. My vlogs are always supposed to be confident, inspirational, and delightfully personal. Viewers know all about me. They want to be me. It's a big responsibility.

My followers only know Miranda from the pics I posted under *My Sister's Fashion Don'ts*. I took those down . . . after.

It wasn't like Miranda was ugly. Quite the opposite. If you looked, you could see the potential, but she just didn't care. Her legs were strong from squatting down behind home plate as a catcher on her softball team. But she refused to listen to my advice about wearing short skirts to show them off. Instead she lived in sloppy hoodies and old jeans. She had this gorgeous mop of naturally curly blond hair, but there were usually huge knots in the back where the brush never touched.

How hard is it to comb your hair? Honestly. For God's sake, put it in a topknot or something.

In preschool once, she put green Play-Doh all over her head. The teacher called and my mom had to go pick her up. Miranda had to get her hair cut to get it all out and it took forever to grow out again. When I asked her why she did it, she said, "Because I wanted to make a mold of my head," like it was the most normal thing in the world. She was weird like that.

I reach out and turn the camera on again.

Tell everyone about Miranda. Tell how this has impacted you.

I talk out loud, but the words aren't planned.

"I would like to thank Your Honor and this court for allowing me to speak today." I pause for a moment to swallow, and then continue. "My name is Torrey Grey and I'm here to talk about my sister, Miranda."

My hands are clenched in my lap, knuckles white. I wish I had something to hold up — a skirt, a bangle, lip gloss.

What could I show? Play-Doh? A moonstone bracelet?

There is a stack of unmarked brown packing boxes that my dad instructed the movers to put in the far corner of the garage. If I were strong enough, I'd go out there, open one, and look at what was inside. I'd haul the pieces of Miranda back to share with everyone in that courtroom and beyond.

Only I'm not strong enough. If I say it all out loud, to a camera or a courtroom or a stupid funeral home boy, I'll start falling inward and I'll never make it out again. All the guilt and pain and sadness will just explode inside my head. I can feel those emotional shards waiting just below my camera-ready shell to cut me into pieces.

And then I'll just end up a walking zombie like my mom.

So I say nothing and the camera keeps filming for another two minutes of silence. Finally, I get out of the chair, turn off the camera, and get into bed. I don't even take my makeup off. It just seems like too much trouble.

Everything is different now. I'm different.

My hand shaking, I reach for the bedside light and snap it off. I roll over onto my back. The walnut four-poster bed seems huge. My eyes slowly adjust to the dark and I watch the shadows of the slowly turning ceiling fan shatter the moonlight across the ceiling.

The clock hits 11:12.

11:13.

11:14.

Close your eyes. You won't go to sleep this way.

When Miranda was little, back when she was afraid of monsters and always came to my bedroom, we played a game. It was from a poem I read to her about being swallowed by a boa constrictor. I'd tell her the snake was eating her toes and then her legs and then her waist. She'd have to relax each body part I talked about and pretend she couldn't even feel it anymore. She was always asleep before I would get to her neck. She thought it was so funny that a snake was swallowing her toes.

But Miranda wasn't a little kid when she died, and it had been a long time since we played the boa constrictor game at bedtime. For the last three years or so, I don't even know what made her laugh. We only communicated by yelling at each other. No silly games and giggles. In the last moments of her life, we were arguing. But I don't want to think about that now.

Feel sleepy. Pretend you can't feel your toes.

Nothing happens. I roll over and face the wall. Random thoughts bounce around inside my brain. Day of the Dead. *Ofrendas*. Skeletons. My teeth clench; my jaw muscles are tight. If I don't go to sleep soon, I'm going to go back to that new school with those ugly purple shadows under my eyes again. The darkness shifts and moves into deeper corners. I glance toward the closed door. There's something moving on the doorframe. In that space between sleep and wakefulness, the hinges turn into dark, slithering snakes, crawling up and down the doorframe.

I'm back in Boulder walking along the outdoor mall. The snow blows hard, swirling away all the other shoppers and faces, until all I see is the window of the store in front of me. The faceless model in the window is wearing a dress. A dress Miranda wore when she was eight — with a full red skirt and white tights that she was always tugging at. The wool hat with the bright red flowers is pulled just low enough on the blank head to keep the nonexistent ears warm, but it is the space between the hat and the dress that I can't stop looking at. The missing face.

Big blue eyes the color of mine. Long, wild blond curls. I can almost hear the laughter coming out of the nothingness. Almost . . .

In the fuzziness of the dream, I put my hand flat against the glass, right up against the girl's face. I close my dream eyes for just a minute but, when I open them, dirt pours in from the ceiling over my body and into my hair. I try to claw my way out. I open my mouth, but instead of air I suck in clumps of sand and dirt. I can't breathe. I wake up to see the door creaking open. Miranda is finally here, but it isn't Miranda. It's a laughing skeleton. Her hands are outstretched, pleading with me.

My eyes fly open. My breath panting. I'm awake. I try to calm my breathing. It is only a dream. Sitting up in the bed, I look over at the rocking chair in the corner of my bedroom. A grinning skeleton rocks away wearing a big flowered hat. She motions to me with one bony finger. It's Blair, the popular princess from school. Every light on the phone in front of her flashes bright red and the buzz of incoming calls grows louder . . . louder . . . louder. I slap my hands over my ears to shut out the noise. All those people wanting something — and going unanswered. Blair, smiling at me, begins to floss her large yellow teeth. As she flosses, the teeth grow sharper, longer, more pointed. Suddenly she is standing in front of me, her thick, honeyed perfume choking me. I try to breathe some spot of air uncontaminated by the sweetness, but it pours into my nose and mouth like a heavy syrup.

It's a dream. Wake up.

"He'll see you now. Go right in." Blair grins a horrible pointy-toothed grin and motions toward the purple door at the end of a long hall. "Don't be late."

I walk toward the door. The hallway stretches out longer with each step. The door is so far away. I begin to run. The door is no closer. I can't be late. I run faster, reaching out for the doorknob. It is so close and then so far away again. I run faster, yet move slower . . . running in deep water. My chest hurts and I am so tired of trying.

Just open your eyes.

Then I'm inside the room. It's a courtroom, and a tall skeleton wearing a big cowboy hat and a black judge robe sits at the head of the table. He motions me toward him. The fluttering pain in my chest grows stronger.

"Recite the capitals of the fifty states," the huge skeleton demands, blinking glassy eyes in my direction.

I begin to recite. "Des Moines, Iowa . . . Oklahoma City, Oklahoma . . ."

The flutter in my chest is so strong I can hardly speak. It bangs against the walls of my rib cage, causing me to jerk and shudder. I keep reciting.

Smaller skeletons in identical hats begin to crawl out of wet, fetid holes in the carpet. One has a camera that keeps snapping pictures with big flashes of light every few seconds.

I know what they want. They want my heart. But it hurts so bad. I can't give it away.

Blair comes in, smiling her pointy-tooth smile, and serves them tiny skulls from a silver platter. They crunch away at them while I just keep reciting, "Juneau, Alaska . . . Little Rock, Arkansas . . ."

You can stop it. Wake up.

Finally I am finished, and the room grows quiet. All the skeletons look at me. The only noise is the banging in my chest. I look down slowly. My skin is transparent. Inside my chest is a moonstone heart. It doesn't beat like a heart should, but glows.

"What do I do?" I ask the now silent row of skeletons.

"You know," the judge skeleton says, "in your heart."

Then he opens his mouth and his pink, snakelike tongue stretches out in one mighty swoop and rips the brilliant, glowing moonstone out of my chest. With a snap and one horrible crunch, it disappears into his mouth.

I wake up for real this time, my heart pounding in my chest and my breath coming in wild gasps. I'm in my bed in the dark and the only sound I hear in the house is the sound of my own breathing. I put my hand on my heart to feel it beating, and breathe in slowly. Once. Twice. My spirit is still inside. I'm alive. Miranda is dead.

Only good dreams . . . only good dreams . . . I whisper. But it doesn't work.

"Watching a haul video is like watching your best friend open their birthday presents." **—Torrey Grey, Beautystarz15**

CHAPTER EIGHT

DOS AND DON'TS FOR THE PERFECT POUT

Mrs. Vardeman, the English teacher, turns off the overhead lights and turns on the projector. She's showing us some poem in a PowerPoint presentation. But it's all I can do to keep my head propped up on my hand and my eyes half open.

For the last few days, my nights have been filled with skeleton nightmares and my mornings crammed full of Raylene talking and talking and talking. This morning, she talked about some guy who makes the best, blingy-est twirling outfits in town when it's not hunting season. Then she had to pull the car over to hug Mrs. Berry, who has some new scents of Poo-Pourri on the market. Raylene is evidently a BIG hugger. That took at least five minutes, but I think I fell asleep in the passenger seat waiting for her to come back, so I don't know exactly.

Luis is sitting in his usual seat in the back. He hasn't spoken to me since I went to his house, which is fine by me. I glance in his direction to see him lean over and say something to the short girl who always sits next to him. She laughs out loud, showing a mouthful of braces. It makes me annoyed. Probably because I'm so tired.

Mrs. Vardeman shuts off the projector and turns the lights back on. "I thought writing your own poem about one of your classmates would be a great way to get to know each other a little better," she announces, and there is a chorus of groans. "So pair up, interview your partner, and write a brief poem about him or her. Then I'll ask you to use the poem to introduce your partner to the rest of us." Mrs. Vardeman hands a stack of papers to the girl in the front row, who begins to pass them out. "Sound good?"

No, it sounds terrible.

"Can we meet with our partner after school for a little *research*?" Ross asks, grinning widely at Blair.

"Sounds like a great idea," the teacher says.

Blair rolls her eyes. "Like *that's* going to happen."

"Okay, everyone, pair up. And try to find out something new about your partner that will surprise us all." Mrs. Vardeman claps her hands together like she's at a birthday party and just received all the presents. I scowl at her, crossing my legs and swinging a foot impatiently. I'm not happy about this forced attempt to foster classroom community.

Kids scramble to pick best friends or crushes. I look around for one last unpopular straggler without a partner. No luck. Luis is matched up with the short girl. Even Raylene has a partner. I'm left with . . .

Blair is standing in front of me. My swinging foot goes still. This is definitely a surprise. What happened to her besties?

"Looks like you're my partner," she says. Her two constant shadows, Mia and Emily, look as astonished as I am by this selection. They hover anxiously behind her, and then quickly scoot two desks over as close as possible to monitor the situation.

"I think I need to know someone who's wearing the Steve Madden buckle boots I've been craving for months," Blair adds, gesturing to my shoes.

"Okay," I say, and she scoots a desk around to face mine. She sits down, unzips a purple backpack quickly, and pulls out a notebook and a pen. Up close, her dark skin is perfectly clear, and her eyelashes so thick and curled they almost touch the bottom of her brows. I'm thinking CoverGirl LashBlast mascara, but I don't ask. She makes me nervous, but I can hide that. It's definitely showtime.

"You first," she says. "Get to know me." It's more of a command than a request.

I look down at the questions Mrs. Vardeman passed out for prompts. "What is your favorite food?" I start.

"Twizzlers."

I don't think that's technically a food, but I write it down anyway.

I read off the next prompt. "What's your favorite saying?"

"Is that really the question?"

I nod, looking over my shoulder. The short girl is laughing at something Luis said.

Blair thinks for a minute, twisting one strand of black hair around and around her finger. "Don't touch my hair, phone, face, or boyfriend," she finally says.

I blink. She's serious. "I'll remember that," I say, and write it down.

"Now you," she says, and leans forward in her chair, so close I get a whiff of Calvin Klein's Euphoria. "Why did you move here?"

"That's not on the list of questions," I say.

"I'm being creative. That's what poetry is all about." She puts the end of the pen in her pink-glossed mouth and waits for me to respond.

"I know you haven't had time to finish," Mrs. Vardeman calls out, and I look toward the front of the room, "but we only have a few minutes before the bell."

I breathe a sigh of relief. Hooray for bad lesson planning.

"Anybody have anything to share about their partner before we leave for today?" Mrs. Vardeman scans the room. There are no volunteers. "Blair, how about you?" the teacher asks.

"I didn't volunteer."

"But I'm sure you have something wonderful to say about your partner." Mrs. Vardeman smiles encouragingly, and Blair rolls her eyes. She stands up, holding her paper out in front of her. The page is completely blank.

"Torrey Grey's eyes are blue," she pretend-reads. She glances over at me and then continues, "Full of secrets hid from view."

Her unexpected insight makes me nervous. There's more to Blair than I first realized.

Blair sits down as Mia and Emily clap enthusiastically.

"That's not exactly the format we talked about, but you are certainly poetic. I'm sure you'll get the idea before Monday, when it's due." Mrs. Vardeman says. "And remember, everyone, next week's quiz is on poetic structure."

The response is a collective groan as the bell rings.

I stand and gather up my things.

"Not in the mood for running this week?" Luis asks, coming up beside me. His tone is casual but his brown eyes are intense. "I haven't seen you on the track."

I catch sight of Blair over his shoulder, hanging by the door with Thing One and Thing Two. Watching. I make a point of frowning.

"I'm kind of busy." My voice is a little too loud, but I want to make sure Blair hears me. "But thanks anyway."

"Maybe some other time," Luis says.

I know Blair can hear everything.

"We'll see," I say, hoping he'll get the picture, and grab my bag to go. I have to push through the group of girls to get out the door. "Sorry. I'm going to be late for my next class."

"Well aren't you just the queen of mean," Blair says behind me.

"Hey, that rhymes. Maybe that should go in your poem,"

Mia says. Emily snorts and then starts giggling. I grin. Blair may not know it yet, but I can match her every step of the way.

I'm already out in the hall and walking away, but Blair's little rhyme pulls a trigger and, in a flash, I remember.

From the very beginning of that horrible day, we were arguing. Probably like most sisters. Zoe always fought with her older sister, too.

"You are the queen of mean," Miranda said. I was trying to get her to hurry up eating her breakfast so we wouldn't miss the next bus to the mall.

"Stop sorting the marshmallows and just eat the cereal," I snapped. I was already stressed with getting everything ready for the on-site shoot. Now her dawdling was going to make me late.

There was one pile of blue moons and another of tiny pink hearts sitting out on the kitchen table beside her bowl of Lucky Charms.

"You don't have to be in such a panic. All those stupid clothes will still be there," Miranda said, then stuffed a handful of stars into her mouth. She narrowed her eyes suspiciously, chewing. "Why do you want me to go so bad anyway?"

I promised Zoe she'd be in every shot — no behind-the-scenes supporting roles for her today — and she was thrilled. But I didn't want to tell Miranda my plans for her to film. Not now, when she could still refuse to go. So I tried to change the subject.

"Eat your cereal. We're going to be late."

If only she had slowed down just a little bit more. Maybe three more bites.

"Make me." Miranda looked at me and grinned. She had smushed all the blue marshmallow moons from her cereal into her front teeth for effect.

"It's not funny, stupid!"

"Torrey!" Mom called from the bedroom. "Don't call your sister stupid."

Miranda mocked me with a pantomimed laugh, careful to not make any actual noise that my mom might overhear.

"Miranda," I pleaded. "Come on. The bus is going to be here any minute."

If only we'd missed the bus.

She finally slid out of the chair and grabbed the backpack I was holding out to her. One of her black Keds was untied and she went down on one knee to tie it with excruciatingly slow movements meant to infuriate me. It was a well-honed talent and, of course, it worked.

"Get outside," I hissed, shoving her out the door in front of me.

"Okay. Okay. Don't push." She swung her stained backpack up over her shoulder. "I'm going."

The bus was rounding the curb. We were going to make it. I was relieved.

If only we had missed the bus.

When we arrived at the mall, things got worse.

"I left my book at home," Miranda said, pawing through her battered backpack frantically. She was really into graphic novels, which were mostly just the same as comic books as far

as I was concerned. I told her those kind of books were for boys. She didn't care.

"It's not like it's even a real book." I grabbed her arm and pulled her toward the shops.

She stopped. "I'm going home."

"The bus going back that way won't be here for twenty minutes," I said. "I'll buy you another book."

"They don't sell that one here. It's special. Not like your stupid earrings or eye shadows," she snapped.

"Miranda, please," I said. "Zoe is waiting. Come on."

Miranda scowled and stomped off to park herself on a bench, digging through her backpack for her sketch pad.

Zoe came out a shop door with an armful of bags, wearing a purple tee and capris. She piled the purchases on the ground next to my feet, then dug around in her Coach bag for her pink flip cam. "Where's Miranda?"

I make a shushing noise, glancing around to see if Miranda could hear. "I haven't asked her yet," I whisper.

"You promised." Zoe froze with the camera in her hand.

"I know. I know. Just give me a minute." I walked over to Miranda's bench.

"You can just prop it up," Miranda said, not looking up. She knew all along what I was going to ask.

"Just do it, Miranda. It's not that difficult."

"Is that lipstick tested on animals?" She nodded toward one of the bags on the ground at Zoe's feet.

"How would I know?" I asked, frustrated. I should have just said no.

Miranda's attention went back to the open art pad, and she looked up only long enough to give me a quick frown. "Then it's not going to happen," she said.

"You promised," Zoe whined behind my back.

I waved an open palm at Zoe. "Don't worry. She'll do it. Give me a minute. Just go scope out the best lighting." I turned back to my sister. "Miranda . . ." I pleaded with her, getting angrier and angrier that I had to beg.

This time she didn't even look up at all. "Busy. Don't care. Not doing it."

"Please," I said, between clenched teeth. I glanced over at Zoe, who was already filming some of the background shots.

"Do you know you can support a bonobo for one year on what that one bag of makeup costs?" Miranda said, standing up.

"I don't know and I don't care," I said.

"You should," my sister said, in that oh-so-judgmental twelve-year-old voice.

I had hit my limit. I grabbed Miranda by her shoulders, shook her, and screamed right into her face, "Grow up, Miranda."

Then she left, stopping only to yell that she was going home.

And those were the last things we said to each other.

But you don't know it's the last thing you're going to say when you say it. If you did, you would probably say something completely different.

"Don't have an opinion? Don't worry. If you watch long enough, you will." —**Torrey Grey, Beautystarz15**

CHAPTER NINE
SURVIVE THE FASHION TRENCHES WITH STATEMENT TEES

My brush-off of Luis in English must have been the right thing to do. At lunch, as I'm standing in the cafeteria, looking for where to sit, Blair materializes by my side.

"Come sit with us." It's not really an invitation, more like a command, but I'm ecstatic to follow her over to the prized spot. I'm in! Mia glares at me when I sit down next to her, but doesn't say anything.

"Hey," says Ross, and I nod at him. He reaches across the table to dip a chicken nugget in Blair's ketchup and she swats his hand away, laughing. He grins at me and pulls his *Don't Mess with Texas* baseball hat a little lower on his head.

I can already tell Ross's signature is constant jokes, wide grins, and baseball hats with changing slogans. Everyone seems to laugh around him. Even teachers. Sometimes they even laugh before he finishes talking because they just expect everything that comes out of his mouth to be funny. It's his thing and he plays it to the max.

"I see you've given up on jackets," Mia says, looking me up and down. Our eyes meet and I don't look away.

I smile brightly. "But I see you haven't given up on fake tans."

Mia gives me a dirty look and I kind of want to stick my tongue out at her. That's what she gets for being a hater. The snappy comeback makes me feel more like myself. This was the me before Miranda's death, and it feels good to be back.

Ross practically spits his milk out all over the table. "Meow," he says, and swipes across the table at me like his hands are claws.

"Joke!" I say quickly. The balance between confident and friendly has to be just right. "I was joking."

Smile. Laugh. Play to the camera.

But Mia doesn't laugh.

"Oh, come on now, Mia. You have to admit Torrey has amazing style." Blair puts one arm around me and squeezes. I'm shocked, and sit there still as glass until she lets go. I try to wrap my head around the idea that I might actually have friends again and that they might even be the popular crowd.

Emily pipes up to echo Blair. She's good at that. "I think you always look fantastic," she says to me. "I would never think of putting together that top with that skirt. Sooo cute. Where did you get it?"

I glance down at my white eyelet skirt and my button-down blue shirt. "Forever 21, I think," I say, trying to remember. "It's been a while since I wore this skirt. In Colorado, we'd be wearing sweaters and boots by now."

"It's horrible." Blair frowns, shaking one of Ross's French fries in my direction for emphasis. "We can never wear fall clothes around here until at least the end of October. Sometimes even later."

"Maybe we'll get a cold front before Halloween. If we're lucky," Emily chimes in. "And then you can only wear fall clothes for, like, two weeks, so you have to make the most of it before it gets hot again."

I nod and sip my soda.

Does everyone talk about the weather?

I glance over at Blair. "Cute bag," I say. "Fossil?"

She nods, patting the smooth brown leather. I can't help but think it's so different than Miranda's brown, beat-up canvas backpack. She took it to school every day, broken straps, pen stains, and all. I told her it looked like something a Cub Scout would wear on a camping trip. I asked her if she *wanted* kids to make fun of her. I even offered her a cute plaid messenger bag to wear in its place. It didn't matter. She wore the stupid thing everywhere.

All of a sudden, Blair is looking over my shoulder and making a face. I turn around and see Luis walking into the cafeteria. He's with some other boys I recognize from other classes of mine. So I guess he's not a total outcast.

"Look, it's Frankenstein," Blair says, elbowing Ross. "He probably even smells like rotting flesh by now."

"Or formaldehyde." Emily holds her nose.

I know for a fact he sort of smells like cinnamon, but I don't say anything.

"You didn't used to think he was such a monster," Mia says to Blair, and I look back and forth between them. I want to ask what that means, but Blair is giving her this scary look like she's said something forbidden, and Mia quickly says, "Sorry."

I look toward Ross for an explanation, but he's looking at Luis, too. I'm surprised to see all traces of his usual grin gone. But then he sees me looking and quickly twists his features back into a smile.

Luis and the other guys disappear out the side of the cafeteria and the table goes back to normal.

"I like your bag, too," Blair says to me, as if there were never any change in the conversation. "And your top. I've seen it before."

She gives me a look, her eyebrows raised, and I feel a rush of nerves. I manage a smile. "Oh, it was everywhere last spring."

"I got it." Blair suddenly snaps her fingers in front of my face. "I know why you look so familiar."

I blink. My throat feels like I swallowed something burning hot. My heart thumps once, hard. Here it comes.

She knows.

"Wait. I'll show you." Blair fumbles frantically in her bag and pulls out her phone, tapping away quickly at the screen. I wait, knowing what's coming. She holds out her phone at arm's length so everyone at the table can see the video playing on the screen.

My voice chirps from the speaker. "Hey, Beauty Stars! I'm Torrey Grey, a fifteen-year-old beauty guru who can tell you all the best styles and trends."

I should leave, but I can't. I'm frozen, watching the train wreck happen. I must make some sort of noise, because Emily looks at me. Then they are all looking at me. My back stiffens and I brace myself for the onslaught.

"Hey . . ." Ross looks away from the screen to me and then back again. He points at the video. "That's you."

"You're on YouTube," Emily says in awe. "Oh. My. God. You're THAT Torrey Grey. Beautystarz15."

Somehow I find words. "That's me," I say, trying to sound casual.

Breathe. Smile. Play to the camera.

"You remember, Mia?" Blair says, waving the phone under her friend's nose. "You showed me her channel last summer. The boho-bun tutorial?"

Mia is the only one at the table who doesn't look shocked by the big reveal. Suddenly, I know without a doubt this is who put the note in my backpack. She recognized me from day one. "Yeah," she says sullenly. "Big surprise."

"Wow. Look at your subscriber count." Blair sounds impressed.

I don't know what to say, so I just sit there with a fake smile plastered on my face.

"I can't believe you're here. In person." Emily breathes, her eyes huge.

"Why *are* you here anyway?" Mia asks, in a tone that indicates she's less than thrilled by my presence.

"My dad transferred. New job." I don't add, *Oh, and by the way, my sister died*. I figure that's the thing coming next anyway, so I wait.

But Mia's next question isn't about Miranda. "So what do you think of these shoes, Beauty Guru?"

She sticks her foot out from under the cafeteria table so I can get a good look at her jeweled sandals. Lots of bling. Totally wrong with those print capris.

"Well . . ." I say, stalling for time and trying to figure out what the right answer is supposed to be. I'm not used to giving a fashion assessment on the spot, face-to-face, or critiquing someone who can actually talk back.

Blair frowns. "Leave her alone, Mia."

Mia holds up her hand. "I just thought she'd want to share some of her expertise with the rest of us."

"They're great," I finally say. "Super stylish."

"I told you," Blair says. "They're perfect. Even Beautystarz15 likes them."

"I'd totally wear them," Ross says. Emily giggles.

I did it. I'm me again. Back where I belong.

I take another bite of my bagel. So people know who I am. It's okay. In fact, it's good. It's better.

Lying in bed that night, I think about what happened in the cafeteria. I try to imagine what will happen when they all find out about Miranda. Will Blair turn out to be just like Zoe, my "best friend," who hasn't been in touch once since I moved away?

I turn over on my back and stare up at the ceiling.

I have to keep Blair on my good side. I don't want to end up shunned, in the same social category as Luis.

Then, even though I don't want to, I think about Luis. I think about his nice hair, black and thick. I think about his face, usually so serious. And I think about his eyes, because when he does smile, it transforms all the darkness. Like a light you turn on and back off again. On — it's brilliant, intense. Then *snap*, the smile is gone again. Just like that.

The pillow feels wrong. I rearrange it, punching it a few times and turning it over. I glance at the clock. It's late. I should have been asleep a long time ago, but there's a now familiar dread inside me, smack in the center of my chest. The nightmares and skeletons are waiting for me to close my eyes.

Tonight, the shadows of this strange room bring a new urge — a craving so powerful I can't ignore it. I want to see something, feel something, of Miranda's. Something she loved. Like shoes and dresses and earrings. Like the things I brought home from shopping trips and held up to the camera to share with my virtual, imaginary friends. Only, the things Miranda loved would be different.

Finally, at two o'clock in the morning, when the rest of the house is asleep, I creep out to the garage. In the top of the second box I find a brown beat-up backpack. It feels smooth and worn under my fingers. Miranda loved this backpack and, if I knew how, I'd give it to her again.

I quietly take it back to my bedroom and stuff it into the dark back corner of my closet. It's my first *ofrenda.*

TORREY GREY'S LAST CONVERSATION WITH DEAD SISTER: YOUTUBE STAR'S RANT POSTED ONLINE

By Laura Collins, MediaBling News, September 20, 2:14 PM MDT

Torrey Grey (Beautystarz15), a popular teen beauty vlogger, is the subject of a new video that features her in a less-than-positive light in the minutes before her sister, Miranda Grey, was tragically hit by a speeding car. Miranda later died at the hospital from her injuries.

The video shows the two girls involved in a heated argument, with Grey yelling at her younger sister to "Grow up" when Miranda refuses to film the footage for Grey's latest haul video. Guru gossip sites have responded with rants trashing the Colorado native.

"Be the person they know and want to be."

—Torrey Grey, Beautystarz15

CHAPTER TEN

CAT EYELINER FOR BEGINNERS

There is a big gray cat face between me and the computer screen.

"He's still looking at me," I complain.

Stu, Raylene's cat, stares back at me with unblinking green eyes. Raylene and I are supposed to be studying for our English quiz, but neither one of us is into it. All I'm focused on at the moment is that my fastest Internet connection in weeks is currently being blocked by a cat.

"He *loves* you." Raylene lies on the floor of her bedroom, with a newspaper spread out in front of her. She is obsessed with the contest going on in the Huntsville *Item* to select the animal models for next year's Humane Society calendar. Every day, she checks the two-page spread of dog, cat, and bunny pictures for the current vote total. So far Stu is not in the top twelve and is, therefore, not in the running to make the calendar. That doesn't stop Raylene from calling faithfully every single day on our way home from school to enter the special dial-in code on her phone to vote for Stu.

It also doesn't stop her from talking smack about all the front-runners.

"Oh. My. God. That Dalmatian is STILL in the lead!" she cries. "He has to be cheating," she adds for at least the tenth time since I've been here. "There is no way one thousand twenty-three people like that black-and-white spotted thing. You watch. He's going to make the month of January. By cheating!"

Stu's tail twitches back and forth across the keyboard — the only thing moving on his huge chunk of a body. It isn't that I don't like cats. I've just never been around one before. Miranda had a hamster once, but that was the only pet we ever had. It was pretty easy to ignore. Stu, not so much.

"Shoo," I whisper. Stu blinks, but doesn't budge. I try to look around him to see the computer screen. He tilts his head to one side and stares solemnly at me, once again completely blocking my view of the monitor. Stu — 1, Me — 0.

Raylene sighs behind me.

"I think Dalmatians are cute," I remark. I know that comment will annoy Raylene, and I'm not disappointed.

"*Cute*? You think black dots everywhere are *cute*? I hear they even have black dots inside their mouths. That is *not* cute. It's disgusting."

I just need a few minutes. Just a quick look at my Google Alerts, if I can keep Raylene occupied with the newspaper contest. I reach out slowly toward Stu. He stares unblinking at me as my index finger gets closer and closer. Then I poke him. Very lightly. On the head.

"Hhhrumph," says Stu, and he gets up, but he just makes a big circle on the desk and then plops back down. Facing the computer screen. Now I am staring at the back of his head.

"Even that stupid cocker spaniel is in the running." Raylene is still talking behind me.

I roll my chair over to one side and try to look around Stu's fat, furry back. I scroll up to the toolbar and type in my name. Pages and pages of mentions. The movement on the screen catches Stu's attention. His head follows the cursor across the screen.

"This is horrible! The freakin' rabbit has more votes than Stu!"

I slide the cursor up to the top of the screen. Stu looks up. I move it to the bottom of the screen. Stu looks down. I move it in a big circle. Stu's head goes around in a big circle. It's kind of entertaining until he reaches out and whacks the screen with a big paw, claws outstretched. I jerk backward in surprise and Stu jumps off the desk with a loud thump.

"I can't even look at this anymore. It's totally wrong." Raylene gathers up the paper in disgust.

"I don't think cats are supposed to thud when they land," I say, watching Stu stalk off toward his bowl of Mr. Purrfect cat food in the corner.

"He needs a new picture. The one they have just doesn't do him justice." Raylene pulls out her phone and snaps a few shots of Stu munching away. He never looks up. "You hold him and I'll take his picture," she says.

"No," I say quickly. The most recent news story with

my name listed on it is all I see. My hands freeze on the keyboard.

It has to be a mistake. Zoe wouldn't have done this.

Raylene scoops Stu up and carries the struggling cat over to the desk. Dropping him into my lap, she steps back and raises the camera to her face.

"Stop, Raylene." I push the cat out of my lap. Reaching over, I grab the phone out of her hand and slam it down on the desk. I'm so focused on the words in front of me, I don't care about Raylene or the stupid cat anymore. All I care about is the screen.

This can't be happening.

I feel a rush of panic as I read the news item. Everything is unraveling. Zoe recorded my last conversation with Miranda, then posted it for the world to see.

I click on the video and all my horrible, angry words spill out into the room. Then I hear my sister's voice and I see her face. For the first time since that day.

It's there. It's real. The memory that has lived inside my head for so long now lives on the Internet. For the whole world to see.

The video ends and the room is silent. I can't breathe.

"Wow," Raylene says after a minute. She reaches for my shoulder and squeezes. "That was horrible. I'm so sorry."

"Shut up," I mumble, hurriedly shutting the browser. I want to run and hide. No. I want to call Zoe and scream at her. No wonder she hasn't returned my messages. She's been busy editing and sharing a video of the worst day of my life.

"Who posted that?" Raylene asks after a long moment.

"A friend," I answer automatically, still reeling from the shock.

"Doesn't look like a friend to me."

"She isn't anymore." I'm trembling as I turn away from the computer and put my head in my hands. There's nothing I can do now. The video is out there. A video that should have never existed.

"Your sister was cute." Raylene pats my back with one hand, but I brush it off.

"Shut up, Raylene!" I say again. I feel bad speaking to her that way. But my mind is whirring, my blood roaring in my ears.

Raylene backs up a few paces, frowning. "I'm sorry. I don't even know what to say."

"Just be quiet." Zoe did this. My best friend. My used-to-be best friend. Who does such a horrendous thing? *What is wrong with her?*

But it isn't just about Zoe. I was the one shouting those horrible things to my sister just before she died.

What is wrong with me?

"Look, I understand. I wouldn't want to talk about it, either." Raylene walks back to her bed, flops down on her stomach across the purple flowered bedspread, and watches me cautiously. Somehow she manages to keep her mouth zipped shut.

I blink rapidly. When this gets out to everyone at school, if it hasn't already, Raylene will likely be the only person who will talk to me. All of my plans for a new life and new friends will never work out.

"I'm sorry," I finally say, turning to Raylene. "I'm not mad at *you*."

"I know," Raylene says. "It must be so hard to think about that day and this" — she points to the computer screen — "makes you remember it all." Her eyes fill up with tears.

I nod. I'm too numb to cry. "That day was such a blur," I say softly. "I rode in the ambulance with her, but she never regained consciousness. By the time my parents got to the hospital she was already in surgery. But it was no use. . . ." I shake my head. "I try not to remember that we argued. But now it's going to be everywhere. This makes me look horrible." Now the tears feel like they will come. I swallow hard.

"Brothers and sisters fight," Raylene says. "It happens. It just makes you more real."

"It's more than that." I pause, trying to put it into words for the first time. "Being real means that everyone can criticize who you *really* are. Not just what you look like."

Raylene looks over at me suspiciously. "But when you do the statement thing for your family, you can tell everyone how sorry you are, right? With all this publicity, there'll probably be tons of reporters in court, and even *more* people will follow your blog."

"Yeah," I say. As the word comes out of my mouth, I feel a tiny spark of hope. The victim impact statement is really the only hope for redemption on the scale I need. Now I know I have to do it.

"Maybe I should do a blog on twirling," Raylene says, her mind as random as the kamikaze squirrels we have so far managed to miss on our daily drive to school. For once I'm almost grateful for her haphazard train of thought. It distracts me from the video I've just seen. At least for a minute.

Raylene picks up the baton off the floor by her bed and waves it at me. "They only pick seven girls, and the competition is tough. If I make it *this* fall, I have to practice all spring before I actually get to go on the field and perform next fall. It's a huge commitment. Jessica Peldrum's older sister, Shannon, was on the line for two years. She got cut her senior year. Really messed up her self-esteem."

I try not to focus on the word *sister*. Instead, I try to think about twirling. Twirling is a safe thought, one that won't make me cry. I know, thanks to Raylene's never-ending chatter in the car, that her hands are swollen from hours of baton twirling. I know the light fixtures in her bedroom and the dining room are smashed because of the twirling. I also know Raylene twirled in the bathroom, and once tried to twirl in the car. Thankfully, the car twirling has never happened again since I've been riding with her and insisted she leave the baton on the backseat.

Raylene sits up on her elbows. "So is it hard?" she asks.

"Twirling?" I ask, my head still spinning.

"No, vlogging."

"Not really. I just sit in front of a camera and talk about my favorite things." I smile at the memory of better times. "It made me feel special. Important."

Raylene thinks over my words for a minute, then finally says, "That's exactly how I feel about twirling."

"So multiply that feeling by a million people all liking you from the Internet and that's kind of what it feels like." I struggle for something to make her connect with the bigger picture.

"Or hating you," she says, and I realize she understands better than I expected.

There is an awkward silence, and then Raylene says, "I'm thinking about having a Halloween party."

I blink at the change of subject.

"And you'll come, right?" she asks.

"Okay," I say. It's not like I'm going to have anything better to do once everyone sees this video.

"You don't have to wear a costume, but you can if you want," she says. "Maybe you could get Blair, Mia, and Emily to come, too?"

"Sure," I say, but I doubt they would come to a party hosted by Raylene. They probably won't want to be seen with me, either. At least not until after I talk in court.

When I get home from Raylene's, I'm surprised to see Dad sitting at the table. He's eating a peanut-butter sandwich with the still-open jar sitting next to him.

"Where have you been?" he asks.

"Raylene's," I answer. All I can think about is the video.

All I can hear is my screaming voice and all I can see is Miranda's angry face.

"Make yourself a sandwich, sweetheart," Dad says, and the warmth in his voice makes me want to run to him, to tell him everything and cry. Instead, I take a deep breath and pull two pieces of bread out of the wrapper on the counter. My parents were fine with me vlogging, but they never really understood. Now they don't even go on the Internet at all. How could I explain the video to my dad?

I slide the slices of bread into the toaster and push down the lever, knocking a small white square off the fridge. I turn it over and stare down at a picture of a blond-haired girl dressed as a scarecrow. She is standing beside a huge orange pumpkin and grinning widely at the camera. I put it back, tucking it a bit more securely under one of the watermelon-shaped magnets. Miranda, age eight.

"How was your business trip?" I ask Dad, turning toward him while I wait for the toast.

"Fine." He takes a bite and chews, staring off into space. His summer tan is fading. No more softball games. Miranda used to play catcher and he was her biggest fan, dragging us all to the games.

"Get in front of it," my dad would yell from behind the backstop. "Don't let it get past you."

I never played sports, so I would just sit in the stands and watch. But I understand wanting to get out in front of things. Like now. I need to do damage control.

I think back to Miranda on the softball field. The pitcher's arm flying around her head and the ball hurtling toward Miranda's waiting glove. My sister never even flinched. The bat would swing just inches from her, connecting to the ball with a loud crack. Then she'd throw off her face mask to focus on a high, pop-up foul ball. Everyone in the stands, even me, held their breath while she tried to put her glove in exactly the right spot for that ball to fall into her hands. And it did. Just like that. Everyone let their breath out in one long rush of air and then clapped and cheered like crazy. Especially my dad.

"Where were you?" I ask him now. I can never keep up. He travels all the time, going to different banks, doing something with their accounts. It all blurs together after a while. Philadelphia? Sacramento?

"Chicago," he says.

"Okay," I say, pulling the bread out of the toaster and joining him at the table. He hands me the knife off his plate, still coated with peanut butter, then reaches out to tuck a strand of my hair back behind one ear. It's been so long since he's done that. I look down at the plate in front of me to hide the sudden rush of emotion.

He frowns. "Are you okay? You look tired."

"I'm fine," I say quickly. Spreading the peanut butter on my toast becomes a very necessary task.

"Maybe you should see someone. A doctor or something. I know all this . . . change . . . is hard."

I glance up at him. "What kind of doctor?"

"Someone you can talk to about everything."

He's serious. A shrink?

"But I have you to talk to," I say, even though I can't remember the last time we've spoken one-on-one like this. "By the way," I add, knowing this change of subject will distract him, "can you take me to the DMV for my driver's license test?" I say it all in a rush so he doesn't have time to say no right away. "If I get a license, it'll really help Mom to not have to drive me . . . everywhere."

The truth is Mom hasn't driven anywhere since Miranda's death. We both know that. And she doesn't want me driving, either. And as much as the idea of driving scares me now, I don't want to keep relying on Raylene for the rest of high school.

Dad blinks at me from behind his glasses. "I don't know," he says, as if he's actually thinking about it. "What does Mom say?"

"She said to talk to you." She didn't, actually, but I wasn't getting anywhere with her on the subject. I take a big bite of the peanut-butter sandwich and chew.

"Let me mull it over," he says finally.

The back door opens and Mom comes in with a basketful of tomatoes. Strands of windblown curls have escaped her ponytail.

"This may be the last of them," she says, putting the basket down on the countertop. "Weatherman says cooler temperatures coming the end of next week. They're calling it a Blue Northern. Funny name, don't you think?"

A tomato rolls off the top of the pile and lands on the kitchen floor with a splash of color. Mom stops talking, frozen by the red stain rolling across the floor.

I jump up from the table, grabbing a couple of paper towels from the rack by the sink.

"It's okay, Mom." I scoop up the tomato and get on my hands and knees to wipe up the mess. Her feet don't move from in front of me. I glance up. Her face is expressionless, her mouth slightly open, her eyes staring at the floor where the smashed tomato used to be.

"Really, it's fine. Look. It's all gone," my dad says, getting up from the table. He puts his arms around her shoulders and tries to pull her stiff body in for a hug.

"It's just such a waste," she mumbles, still staring at where the red stain used to be.

Without saying anything, I leave the kitchen. I need to be alone.

In my bedroom, I immediately pull out my phone and look up the video. But I see that it's been taken down. By the website? By Zoe? There are tons of comments, though — people saying I'm awful, people saying the video is awful. I can't read them. I shut off my phone and close my eyes.

I know I should feel relieved the video is down, but I find myself thinking I desperately want to see it again. For Miranda. Even if we were fighting, she was still there. Talking and moving. I want to see her face, animated and angry. I want to hear her judgmental, opinionated voice.

I miss her.

That night, when I can't sleep, I don't even try to fight the urge. I need these things now more than ever. These are the objects that will guide me in my courtroom statement. Somehow they will lead me back to the Miranda I've forgotten and give me the words to say when the world is watching.

I throw back the sheet and slide out of bed. I make my way to the garage.

But tonight someone is already there before me. My dad is on his knees in front of an open cardboard box. He doesn't even hear me come into the garage. I slide over into the corner behind the car, not wanting to watch, but not able to look away. In his hands is a catcher's mitt. His fists are clenched in the leather, his face contorted with grief. His back heaves with each deep, guttural sob.

The tears rush down my face and I put my hand over my mouth to keep from making any noise. I can't bear to watch. This is private.

It's a long time before Dad puts the glove carefully back into the cardboard box. Stumbling back toward the house, he's oblivious to me standing in the dark corner. I wait until I know he's gone and then I go to the boxes. I pull out the glove and take it back to my room.

"If you don't like a video, stop watching. Don't spend hours bashing it." **—Torrey Grey, Beautystarz15**

CHAPTER ELEVEN
TEN WAYS TO STAY TONED

The football team is practicing on the field when I make it out to the track. I recognize Ross as he runs across the twenty-yard line toward the goal post, catching a football over one shoulder and not even breaking stride. I'm impressed. He turns and heads back toward the huddle at a slow trot, grinning widely and acknowledging the whoops of congratulations. He's so focused on practice that he doesn't even look my way.

I also see Raylene in the distance, tossing a spinning baton up in the air over and over again. She misses it three times before she finally catches one. Thank God she doesn't see me as I slip in the side gate and hang out by the fence.

Ever, the green-eyed girl I met in the cafeteria on the first day of school, is sitting alone on the bottom step of the bleachers tying her running shoes. There's no sign of her blond boyfriend with the strange name. She stands and walks down onto the track, lifting a hand in greeting.

"Hey, Torrey."

For some reason I didn't expect her to remember my name. Then I feel a flash of paranoia and wonder if she saw the video over the weekend. If she did, though, she gives no sign of it.

"I'm Ever. I met you in the lunchroom a couple of weeks ago?"

"I remember," I say.

She places both hands on the retaining wall in front of her and leans forward. She bends one leg forward and pushes the other straight back, keeping the heel on the ground.

It looks like she knows what she's doing, so I join her at the wall, stretching out my legs and waiting for Luis to show up.

"You're a runner?" I ask.

She laughs. "Not really. I'm just not a walker anymore."

"I guess we all have to start somewhere," I say.

"What about you?" she asks.

"My first time. But you know what they say," I answer. "Strong is the new skinny. Feature article in last month's *Glamour* magazine."

"I've heard that," she says with a half smile. There's a sudden strange expression on her face, but I don't ask any questions. People have secrets. Of all people, I understand that.

"Well, I better get going if I'm going to finish in time for practice."

"Band?" I ask.

"No, I sing," she says. "See you later?"

I nod, and she starts off around the track at a slow jog. Then I turn to see Luis approaching.

"You changed your mind?" he asks, stopping at my side.

"Oh, hi." I put a hand up to shield my eyes. "I forgot you said you'd be here now."

"Right," he says, and I know he doesn't believe me. "Are you coming or not?"

"Just a minute," I say, and go down on one knee to tie my shoelace. He stands, watching and waiting, as I pull the laces tight.

"I like your fingernail polish," he says. "Cuban Rose?"

"How did you know?" I look up, surprised. I quickly tuck my ugly fingers into my palms, embarrassed that that's the thing he notices about me.

"I watched a couple of vlogs from Beautystarz15. Interesting." I can't tell whether he's making fun of me or not. "It's actually pretty close to the color of a Cuban rose."

"Now you're an expert on flowers?" I stand up and we face each other.

"I know a lot about flowers. Part of the job. Did you know that ancient Greeks introduced the idea of bringing flowers to a funeral to mask the smell?"

I make a face. "That's disgusting."

"Why? Funerals have been around a long time. There's evidence ancient Romans actually hired mourners and arranged services to ease the grief of the families."

"Are you going to run or talk?" I ask.

"Believe it or not, I can do both at the same time." He grins. The light switch flips on — dazzling.

"Lucky me," I say, feeling the heat rush into my face and trying to act nonchalant.

We start off at a trot and I can tell he's totally holding back. At first there is only the sound of the graveled track beneath our feet and the calls of the players out on the field. Luis runs silently beside me and waits, as if he knows I have something on my mind.

"So, I was thinking," I say after only a few steps. I'm breathing deeply out of my mouth, but I'm keeping up and I can still have a conversation without gasping for air.

"About?"

"You know how you said that people collect memory things . . . ?" My voice trails off, but I force myself to keep going.

"Ofrendas?"

I nod. "What do they *do* with them?"

He gives me a quick sideways look, raising his eyebrows. "On *el Día de los Muertos*? Or just in general?"

"Let's start with the Day of the Dead," I answer. It seems easier to talk when my body is occupied.

"Well, the holiday isn't one single day. It's actually several days celebrated in Mexico and around the world." He picks up the pace and I consciously have to make my legs move faster to keep up with him. "On the first night, people think the spirits of dead children, the *angelitos,* are allowed to come back and be with their families for twenty-four hours."

The *angelitos.* It's impossible not to think of Miranda.

We jog around the bend of the track. My breath is already shallow.

Luis talks easily beside me, no sign of sweat or exertion.

"Families spend the night in the cemeteries and put the *ofrendas* out on the grave to welcome the spirits home the moment they are released from heaven."

"You don't believe spirits come back from the dead, do you?" I ask, brushing my hair out of my face with one hand.

"There was this doctor who weighed people right before and right after death. He found that people were lighter right after they died when their spirit left their body." Luis looks over at me, serious. "He said it was proof of the existence of a soul."

"Right," I say cynically. "So exactly how much does a soul weigh?"

"Twenty-one grams, according to Dr. MacDougall."

"And you believe that?"

He shrugs. We jog down the straight side of the track in silence, but I'm thinking.

I see Raylene out on the field, spinning around and around with the baton. She stops long enough to call out to me and wave wildly. I raise my hand in a halfhearted wave. I am eternally grateful she is occupied for the moment *and* that there is no sign of Blair and friends. We run halfway around the track again before Luis says anything else.

"How do you know Raylene?" he asks.

"She's my cousin."

He nods, and we jog on around the bend. My breath is coming in quick gasps.

"She's crazy." I manage to get it out between pants.

"Duh," he says, and laughs. I like the sound of it and find myself laughing with him. Surprises me. I can still laugh.

"Yeah, me and Raylene are going to be best friends," I say, and Luis's smile fades at my sarcastic tone.

"You could do worse," he says.

I change the subject. "How did Mr. Paulson's viewing go the other week?"

"His daughter was surprised by the number of girlfriends. She had no idea her dad was so popular. But there wasn't a big scene, so that was good."

We come around the turn and Ross sprints across the football field again to make another gravity-defying catch.

"He's good," I say.

Now there's no trace of a smile on Luis's face. "Yeah. Lots of natural talent and lots of practice. He's had a ball in his hands since he could walk."

How do you know that? You don't even speak to each other.

Luis's face is hard, closed. I don't ask any questions about Ross.

Instead I ask, "Are you going to take over the family business someday?"

"That's the idea." I glance over at him. His eyes are straight ahead, his expression still solemn. "My older brother already failed the mortuary sciences test twice. He's never going to get his license and it's really not for him."

There's a test?

"But you *want* to do it?" I ask.

"Yeah. I do," he says. "I feel like it's something that I'm . . . not *good at,* because nobody's *good* at it . . . but it's something I can handle. Does that make sense?"

"Not really."

"The way I look at it, I can be strong when someone else can't be. That's pretty important, don't you think?"

"I guess so." Surprisingly, the way he describes it almost sounds cool. Almost. But I know the other side. I know how it feels to walk into a silent house every afternoon. About parents who are falling apart. And what it's like to have dreams that leave you sweating and gasping for breath every night. None of that is cool.

"It seems unhealthy," I say, then realize the irony of me calling him unhealthy when I'm the one gulping in air.

He doesn't comment on that, but says, "It's not the dead that get to me. It's the people left behind. They have a look to them. A gone-missing look." When I don't respond right away, he adds, "They look like something really important has suddenly gone missing and they are searching everywhere for it. But no matter how hard they search, no matter where they look, they can't find it."

He's watching me now and I glance quickly away, a knot in my throat. I know exactly what he's talking about.

It's my mom.

And I worry it's me, too. I always expect Miranda to walk into a room in her softball uniform, to hear her laughing to her favorite cartoons in the other room, to just *see* her. Somewhere. Anywhere.

I'm quiet for a long time.

"She liked animals," I say eventually. "She even adopted one from the zoo with her allowance. She said she was going to be a veterinarian and work at an animal sanctuary when she grew up."

When she grew up.

Grow up, Miranda.

My steps get faster, and I ignore my cramping calves. Luis easily keeps up with me and, to my surprise, I keep talking. "Lately I've been collecting things of my sister's. It helps me remember what she was like."

"Ofrendas," he says.

"Something like that." I see him nod, and I don't say anything else.

We come to a stop at the gate and I'm finally able to catch my breath. Luis stretches out his calves and I peer around to make sure there's no sign of Blair or anyone else that matters.

"I like talking to you." The words slip out before I can stop them and I instantly regret it. This isn't the friendship I'm supposed to encourage. Luis isn't in the plan. He could actually destroy my blueprint for a comeback. I don't want that, do I?

Then the light switch of his smile flips on and I don't regret anything anymore. How can I, when he's smiling at me like that?

"I was thinking," he says. "I have to work every night this week. Lots of people . . ."

"Died?"

"Yeah. Busy week."

"And?" I stop, my hand on the gate.

"How about having lunch with me on Saturday?" he asks. "We can go to La Ventana. It's on the square. What do you say?"

"Yes." Again, I speak before I can even really think. I only know I want the conversation with Luis to continue.

"Great," he says, and the smile stays on his face longer than usual.

I'm suddenly a little worried about meeting up with Luis right in town. Someone from school might see us there. *But it's okay,* I tell myself. At least we're not meeting over an embalming table. Or, worse, at the geek table in the cafeteria.

"I'll meet you there," I say. Hopefully I should have my driver's license by then and won't have to count on Raylene taking me.

"Okay," he says.

I stand there a moment, the sun already starting to heat up my back, as he walks away.

I wonder what my subscribers would think of Luis Rivera. Yes, he's hot, but he works in a funeral home and helps bury people. There is nothing fashionable or glamorous about that.

Then again, there's nothing fashionable or glamorous about what's happening to me, and in my home, right now. I think about the nightmares. About Mom and her tomatoes. What Luis said about the "gone-missing" look.

I watch as he turns the corner and disappears around the brick wall of the gym.

"Try filming in natural light. It'll keep your videos from being too dark." —**Torrey Grey, Beautystarz 15**

CHAPTER TWELVE

DAMAGE CONTROL FOR FLYAWAY HAIR

In the car the next morning, Raylene tells me that Mia's mother is a warden at the women's prison in town and that Blair gets her wardrobe from her aunt, who owns a fancy boutique in River Oaks. She swears she saw a tag tucked into one of the shirts Blair wore to school last week. Raylene's big theory, which she discusses for at least five blocks, is that Blair returns the clothes after only wearing them once, and then her aunt sends her a new batch. Raylene also discusses, with herself, obviously, because I'm not saying anything, if she should wear a cat costume to her Halloween party.

Thank God I'm going to get my license on Friday.

By English, I'm dragging, and I know it's showing on my face when I push down the aisle past Blair. She glances up and nods, but doesn't say anything. No one has mentioned the video of me and Miranda and I've been too big a chicken to check the online gossip sites. The clip is etched into my mind so vividly, I never have to see it again.

As Mrs. Vardeman finishes calling roll, my phone buzzes

in my purse. I pull it out, careful to keep it from sight. I've already witnessed four phones being confiscated by the teacher, and I'm not about to risk the same fate. I glance down at the text message — from Zoe.

My heart jumps.

I'm sorry. CALL ME?

I slide the phone back into my purse, my stomach twisting into a knot. What can I even write back?

Saying you're sorry doesn't make it all okay. Where have you been, Zoe? How could you do something like that to me?

Mia leans over across the aisle, interrupting my thoughts. "I saw you out at the track yesterday."

Oh no. Something else to make my insides squeeze. *Does she mean with Luis?*

"Okay," I say, waiting to see what's coming next. But she's already turned back to talk to Ross on the other side of the aisle. I look over at Luis, but he's pulling out his books and doesn't look in my direction.

Mrs. Vardeman starts the lesson, something about poetic structure, but I can't stop thinking about what Mia said.

Is she trying to intimidate me? Threaten me? Did she tell Blair?

Raylene is waving her hand from the front row, but doesn't wait to be called on. "Is this going to be on the test?" she asks, and Mrs. Vardeman rolls her eyes.

"Yes, Raylene." She turns to address the rest of the class. "And you'll all be ready, right?"

There are scattered moans across the room.

"Fair warning. On this quiz, you'll be expected to recognize several rhyme schemes in examples of poetry." Mrs. Vardeman looks directly at Raylene. "So let's do a quick review. Who can tell me the rhyme scheme for a cinquain?"

Raylene's hand goes down in an instant.

There's silence, and several kids look down at their desks. I glance over at Luis. He's writing something in his notebook.

"Ross?" Mrs. Vardeman gives up on a volunteer.

"A-B-A-B-B," Ross answers.

"Correct."

"And who developed the cinquain in the modern form?"

"Adelaide Crapsey."

You have to be kidding me. That's his name?

"Correct again. Well done, Ross."

We all look at him in surprise. Who knew?

He takes off his baseball hat and sweeps it down over his chest in an exaggerated bow. "And that, kids, is how it's done," he says.

"Oh brother," says Emily, with a toss of her perfectly spiral red ringlets. Blair laughs, and Raylene, on the other side of Ross, high-fives him.

I realize I didn't know the answer to either question. It's a bad sign of how little I've paid attention in class. I need to do better. I try to focus on the review Mrs. Vardeman is giving us now, but my mind keeps hopping between Zoe's text and Mia's remark. How can I concentrate on what's a ballade and a couplet when everything is unraveling?

"You joining us?" Blair asks me as I get in line to pay for lunch later.

I tell myself I might still have a chance. Mia must not have said anything yet or, even better, she didn't see me with Luis.

Who am I kidding? It's just a matter of time now.

I pay quickly, then follow Blair to the table, figuring I should make the most of what little time I have left.

Ross is sitting next to Max Wallace, a guy I recognize from my history class. He has a buzz cut and is wearing a bright green football jersey.

"This is Torrey," Ross says briefly, and Max nods my way before eating the rest of a burrito in three huge bites. Still chewing, he squishes the tinfoil wrapper into a ball and throws it at Ross.

Ross bats it away, and it bounces off Blair's shoulder before landing on the floor. She flinches and squeals like a tiny piece of tinfoil could mortally wound her. Emily giggles and Mia just rolls her eyes.

I have seen Max in the hallways with Ross, but never at the cool table before. Max is now explaining that he spends most of lunch period in the weight room during football season. I think of Luis, but resist looking around the cafeteria for him.

"I'm the kicker," Max is saying to me. "For the football team?"

I nod.

"I used to play soccer, but this guy" — he gestures to Ross — "convinced me that kicking field goals is the real way to fame and fortune."

"Torrey is from Colorado," Blair says to Max, like it's Hollywood or something. I expect him to smirk at me like Mia is smirking now.

But Max leans forward across the table and grins at me. "I spent some time white-water rafting up in Colorado a couple of summers ago," he tells me proudly. He takes a long swig of milk, then wipes his mouth on the back of his hand. "My grandparents live up near Durango," Max goes on. "It is amazing. Must have been hard to leave."

"Yes, it was," I say after a moment.

Max is cute. Back in Colorado, I would have assumed he was flirting with me, and flirted back. Now I don't return his grin. I can't quite say why.

Then Mia turns to me with a question. "What were you doing with Luis Rivera yesterday?"

I knew this was coming, but it still catches me off guard. I feel my face flush.

Ross chews in silence on a slice of pepperoni pizza. Max drinks more milk. Blair and Emily exchange a shocked glance. Mia is giving me a snarky smile. She's only interested in making me look bad in front of Blair, and she knows exactly the button to push. The pressure is on for me to keep my spot at the table, and I'm not about to give up.

"We happened to be running the track at the same time. It was no big deal," I say, trying not to show how uncomfortable I am.

"It sure looked like you had a lot to say to each other." Mia's eyes dart over to get Blair's reaction. I realize this is why she waited to tell Blair until now. She wants my rejection to be public.

"I had some things to talk to him about." I take a bite of bagel and chew, still strategizing about what to say. I swallow, but the doughy bite seems lodged in my throat. I swallow again.

"Like what?" Blair narrows her eyes at me. Mia looks quickly back and forth between me and Blair. She's not happy about Blair's interest in me. I get it. There are only so many spaces at the popular table.

I pull another chunk off the bagel and try to buy some time. By the looks on everyone's faces, I know I'm walking into a field of land mines. I fake cough and then take a drink of milk. My mind is racing. If I say the wrong thing, *boom*, I'm kicked back into oblivion. But what is the *right* thing? I can't very well say I like talking to Luis Rivera. Which is the truth.

"Yeah," Emily pipes up, because she's the parrot of the group. "What were you talking to Luis about?"

Suddenly, I think of an excuse that will get me off the hook and wipe that look right off their faces. I don't want to use it, but I'm desperate.

Just tell them. Say it.

"My sister was killed in an accident right before I moved here." I take a deep breath and continue. "Luis's family helped with the burial of my sister's ashes. I just had some . . . details . . . to discuss with him."

The table goes quiet. Ross freezes with the piece of half-eaten pizza almost to his mouth.

"What happened?" Blair asks. She seems genuinely

shocked, her brown eyes wide with sympathy. For the moment, no one is thinking about Luis Rivera.

"She was hit by a drunk driver." I try to say it casually, but I don't think I've ever said those words out loud before, and my voice shakes a little.

"That's terrible," Blair says. "I'm so sorry."

Everyone at the table is looking at me soberly. Ross makes a sympathetic sound, and Emily pats my arm.

"I think I heard about this," Mia says, and right away I know she knows everything. "You were filming a vlog when it happened, right?"

I don't want to talk about that part at all. I turn away from her to face the others.

"I have to go back to Colorado and talk at the sentencing," I say instead.

"Wow," Max says quietly, sounding impressed.

There's a long stretch of silence at the table.

"So what did you have to discuss with Luis?" Blair finally asks.

I shrug. "My parents wanted me to ask him a question about the cemetery."

"Poor you," Blair says, and I know she means because I had to talk to Luis. I nod, trying to keep my expression neutral.

I settle back and let the noise of the cafeteria conversations blur around me. I'm still here. A part of the group. I did it.

Then a ball of guilt settles in my stomach. I just used my sister's death to stay at this table.

What does that say about me?

"I never get tired of hearing that one of my videos put a smile on someone's face." **—Torrey Grey, Beautystarz15**

CHAPTER THIRTEEN

FALL HAUL: DRESSES TO DRIVE 'EM CRAZY

My dad rolls down the window as I come around the front of the car, dodging some kid with a trombone case running for the bus home.

"You want to drive?" Dad asks.

"No," I say, opening the passenger side and sliding in. I know that will disappoint him, but I'm already regretting the deal we made. I go to the shrink today and he takes me to the DMV on Friday. I figure sitting on a couch for one hour is worth it.

"If you're going to get your license, you really should be practicing."

My dad thinks teaching me to drive should be a bonding experience. He always brings up how his dad taught him to drive and how, even though I finished driver's ed in Colorado and aced my written test, I should drive now and then with him in the car.

I know it's really to check and see if I'm all freaked out behind the wheel now, like my mom is. And I'm not, except

I really don't know that for sure, because I keep saying no every time he asks me to drive.

"I've practiced enough," I say, frowning.

He pulls out of the school parking lot and into the line of cars waiting to turn right at the stop sign. A truck honks loudly behind us and a boy leans out the window to yell something at a half-open bus window.

As he's driving, Dad talks through every move, every decision, like it's rocket science. "Move your right foot from the accelerator over to the brake when you need to stop or slow down. You don't want to be a two-footed driver."

Oh no. I don't want that.

A girl jumps off the curb into the crosswalk, waving and yelling at a friend across the street. My dad slams on the brakes, throwing his hand up in front of me, and we both jerk forward against the seat belts. It wasn't even close, but it leaves us both breathing hard. I know we're thinking about Miranda. How could we not?

Finally, Dad turns right and gets onto I-45.

"How was your day?" he asks.

"Fine," I say, and my tone must have let him know my mood. He doesn't ask any more questions.

I stare straight ahead at the highway stretching out into the late-afternoon sun. If all roads were this empty, it would be easier to relax behind the wheel. Unfortunately, I don't have high hopes the driver's license test will be out on an open, empty highway.

We exit the highway and pull into a shaded parking lot

right off the feeder road. I feel the tension tighten the back of my neck. The discreet sign on the side of the bland brick building in front of the bumper says DR. SONYA SHELLY, MD, ADOLESCENT PSYCHIATRY.

"I know you don't want to do this," Dad says, parking the car.

You think?

"It's fine," I say, still staring out the front windshield. I can tell out of the corner of my eye that he's looking at me. He takes one hand off the steering wheel and gives me an awkward pat on the shoulder.

"I talked with Dr. Shelly last week. I think you're really going to like her."

"Right," I say under my breath.

"Oh, Torrey." Dad sighs. "Just give it a chance."

I get out of the car, slamming the door behind me and leaving him to come in by himself.

Inside; I find the right door at the end of a long hallway. Puzzle pieces are spread out over a wooden table in the tiny waiting room. A box top with a picture of three big red apples is propped up beside the scattered pieces, but nothing among the colored bits on the table looks like apples. The people who waited here before me evidently had enough to think about without trying to fix a stupid apple puzzle.

All the king's horses and all the king's men couldn't put Humpty together again.

My dad appears in the waiting room and sits down across from the puzzle. He gives me an "I'm here for you" smile. I don't smile back. We both sit silently until a woman with frizzy, mousy-colored hair comes out to introduce herself as Dr. Shelly. She's wearing a long flowery skirt, and somebody definitely lied to her when she asked them, *Does this skirt look good on me?*

She has on ugly black comfortable shoes. I instantly think of tweeting a picture of the skirt and the shoes as an example of a fashion DON'T. It makes me smile just a bit to think of the comments and retweets the post would get. The doctor's eyebrows rise in question as she motions me into her office. I don't explain. In fact, I don't say anything at all.

The dark brown couch and the carefully pale paintings of flowers are intentionally boring. I guess no one freaks out looking at dull yellow daisies, right? There's a box of tissues placed strategically on the coffee table.

Yeah, right.

I make a vow right then to not use a single tissue, because it's obvious that she's going to try to make me cry. I'm not about to give her that.

Dr. Shelly motions me toward the couch, but I choose the beige chair instead. Then I stare back at her, focusing on the pupils of her brown eyes.

"You don't have to talk today if you don't feel like it," she says. Her voice is flat, calmed by years of practice talking to crazy people.

Bingo. As a matter of fact, I don't *feel like it*. It feels intensely powerful to be silent.

And that's when it hits me. There are no rules here. Nobody is watching. I don't have to pretend to be nice or charming to her. She's not allowed to tell anyone about me. The spotlight is off. All I have to do is wait her out. I push back into the chair with the realization I'm in control for the first time in a very long time.

"I know it wasn't your choice to come here."

Right again, Doctor. Nothing is my choice.

I don't respond. She doesn't seem uncomfortable with my silence yet but I realize I want her to be, and all of a sudden it's like a competition.

"How are things going in your new school? In your case, everything is being played out in a very public way. How does that make you feel?"

I don't want to think about how it feels. Instead, I think about how people raise their voices at the end of a sentence to indicate they are asking you a question. Just because they ask you something, you don't have to answer. I focus in on her diplomas behind her head. She graduated from schools I've never heard of.

"Your friends may feel frightened by everything that's happened, and try to pull away. It's not that they don't care about you anymore." She pauses. She obviously doesn't understand. How could she?

They don't just pull away. They betray and humiliate me. Publicly. Like Zoe. The thought of Zoe brings unexpected emotion and I instantly push it back down. *Don't cry. Don't cry. Don't cry.*

"Your father told me you are having difficulty sleeping."

I notice the diamond wedding ring on her left hand. Surprisingly larger than I expected. Maybe a carat and a half? And a French manicure. She obviously spends more time at the nail salon than at the hair place. I look back up at her face.

"*Are* you having trouble sleeping?" she asks.

I blink, but don't look away this time. I saw on a television crime show that would be a sign of some reaction.

"Bad dreams?" Dr. Shelley asks. I'm silent. She continues. "Sometimes you can learn things from dreams. Your mind might be trying to tell you something, and the message may be so important it refuses to go away."

What might skeletons in my dreams mean, Doc?

Her mouth is still moving and sound is still coming out. It makes it easier to keep my face bland and expressionless if I don't actually hear the words, so I let them wash over me in sounds that move up and down. Questions. Statements. More questions.

When I do focus in long enough to understand the words, I hear her say things like, "Denial is a common reaction in grief. It's part of pretending nothing happened. It's a way of coping."

And I'm suddenly angry. So angry I could punch her. She doesn't have the right to tell me what my reaction is. Nobody does.

While I wait for her to stop droning on and on, I practice my fierce look. It's where you let your face and mouth go all dead-like and just your eyes are alive. Fierce. It looks great on camera.

Dr. Shelly blows out a sigh between her thin lips. One tiny reaction that satisfies me enormously.

You don't like the quiet game, do you?

And, just like that, I think of nine-year-old Miranda bursting into my room on a late spring afternoon, three years ago.

"I think it's time for the quiet game," I said, but Miranda knew that trick.

"Kaylie Smith asked me to her birthday party this weekend. She's the first in the class to turn ten. It's going to be a carnival theme." She was talking so fast I could hardly understand her. "And there is going to be a face painter there and I think I might get a lightning bolt painted on my face. Not like the Flash. More like Jolt."

"Uh-huh," I said. I had no idea who Jolt was.

"Right here," she pointed to her left cheekbone. "And for lunch today we had rosy applesauce and I think it made me feel sick to my stomach. Do you think I'm allergic to rosy applesauce, Torrey?"

"No," I said, pulling my cell phone out of my pocket to see if I'd missed anything. I was thirteen, had just posted my first vlog, and was eager to see if someone, anyone, had watched it yet. I wasn't thinking about applesauce and superheroes. The only thing on my mind was fame.

"But after lunch I felt better." Miranda wasn't even taking a breath. "And Mrs. Jackson, the art teacher, let us paint with real paints. I think the best color in the world is blue. What do you think, Torrey?"

I didn't answer, looking at my phone. Three people somewhere in the world just watched my vlog. Adrenaline pumped into my body.

"I'm bored. Let's play hide-and-seek. Come on. Please." She was hopping all over my room.

Hide-and-seek.

It was a game we'd played together since Miranda was able to walk. Now that I thought about it, maybe even before then. When she was a baby, I'd throw her blue baby blanket over my head and "disappear." She'd actually cry sometimes at the thought that I'd somehow left her. Or at least she would start to cry until I pulled the blanket off my head and — "ta-da!" — reappeared. Miranda had found me. She would giggle wildly — a baby laugh so contagious everyone in hearing distance would start to laugh, too. She loved that game so much, Mom would make me play it with her over and over again on long car trips. She never tired of it. It was so simple, really, but it never failed to make me feel good, too.

Now I was too grown-up, too cool, to play childish hide-and-seek games, no matter how many times she asked.

"You're too old for that," I told Miranda, looking back at my phone. I had a text from Zoe, telling me she thought my vlog was amazing.

"Nobody's too old for hide-and-seek," Miranda said, and I could tell she wasn't going to go away that easily.

"Okay. You go hide and I'll come find you," I said, glancing up at my sister.

For a quick moment, her face lit up, and then she realized it was just another trick.

"You're not coming to find me, are you?" she said sadly.

I blink, bringing myself back to the present. The guilt I feel inside buzzes like the tiny Texas June bugs beating themselves against Dr. Shelly's office window. Suddenly I can't sit here a second longer.

"Are we done yet?" It's the first thing I've said since I entered the room, and it seems to actually surprise Dr. Shelly. She sits back in her tall black leather chair, the pad empty on her lap.

"Is that what you want?"

No. I want to get a pic of Zoe's latest hairstyle. I want to eat Simply Strawberry gelato at the mall and tweet how delicious it is with fresh mango on top. I want to check my page views. I want to grab Cody's hand and walk through the halls of my old school. I want to shop the coupon sale at Macy's and then post a haul video that gets ten thousand "likes" in an hour.

I want things to be like they were before.

"Yes," I say, and stand up.

When I come back out into the waiting room, Dad goes inside to talk to Dr. Shelly for a few minutes by himself. Later, he lectures me all the way home about my behavior, or lack thereof, with the therapist. Evidently, there is no doctor-patient confidentiality privilege where parents are concerned.

As soon as we get home, I go to my room, slamming the door behind me. I pull out my biology homework and stare at it like it's magically going to make sense. It doesn't.

Eventually I give up and get ready for bed, changing into pajama pants and a tank top. I brush my teeth and crawl under the covers. Then, without warning, something Dr. Shelly said pops into my head. I'd been trying to tune her out, but I must have retained more than I realized.

She'd said that sometimes grief makes you do crazy things. I wonder what she'd say if she knew about the stash of Miranda's things I have in the bottom of my closet.

Is that crazy, Dr. Shelly?

What would she say if I told her I added a drawing of Sensational Sister to the pile last night at one thirty in the morning?

Do you think collecting things of a dead person's is strange, Dr. Shelly?

Luis Rivera doesn't think it's weird. Suddenly I want to talk to him so badly I would call him, but I don't have his number. He didn't talk to me all week at school, and I was somewhat relieved. It allowed me to continue sitting with Blair and Mia and Emily.

But tonight I feel like I could talk to him about anything — *ofrendas,* courtrooms, spirits, nightmares — and I wouldn't even care if Blair was standing right beside us. I hope I still feel that way when I meet him for lunch on Saturday. And that's what I'm thinking about when I finally fall asleep.

But when I wake up just a few hours later, panting from my latest nightmare, all I can think of are the boxes in the garage. The pull is irresistible. It's time to add to my collection.

Stumbling out to the garage, I search through the stack of boxes. Opening up the third one, I uncover a tiny blue baby blanket with a big yellow duck on the front. *Hide-and-seek.* I carefully carry it back to my bedroom and tuck it away inside the backpack in my closet.

"Sometimes people forget I'm just like anybody else."

—Torrey Grey, Beautystarz15

CHAPTER FOURTEEN

CUTE FIRST-DATE LOOKS

I got my license. Somehow, I managed to make it through the driving test without freaking out, and I did it — I can now go where I want, when I want, in a car.

Which is also terrifying.

But I'm determined to drive myself to lunch with Luis. I'm shocked Dad lets me drive the car. If Mom weren't lying down in the bedroom, I know she'd never allow it. But I can tell Dad doesn't want to keep me from meeting a friend, because it's been a while since I've actually had friends to meet. Finally, after some hemming and hawing, he hands over the keys. Before I walk outside, he goes over all the same directions he's already told me a million times, and then he gives me a hug.

I get in the car, feeling a little shaky. I turn the key in the ignition. I'm surprised it starts. Now I have to actually drive. By myself.

I put the car into reverse, squeezing the wheel tightly with both hands, and push down on the accelerator with my right foot. The car lurches backward down the driveway and out into the street. I put it in drive and wave to my dad, standing on the front sidewalk, watching. He frowns and waves back halfheartedly. A little heavy-footed on the brake, I shudder to a hard standstill at the intersection and look both ways. I take a deep breath and turn the blinker on.

It's really only a couple of turns, and there's very little traffic on these streets. I hardly even see another car. I just need to make sure and watch for the road signs. And the speed limit signs.

And watch out for kids in crosswalks.

Don't think how the car looked that day with its crumpled hood. Don't think of Miranda lying broken and unconscious in the street.

There's a parking spot near the square downtown and I inch into it with room to spare on both sides. I turn the car off, my hands trembling, and sit there for a minute trying to calm my thumping heart.

You're fine. You did it. Nothing happened.

After a few minutes, I look in the mirror, checking my reflection. I pinch my cheeks to bring back some color and quickly finger-comb my hair. The woman getting in the car next to me looks at me curiously. It's probably strange to see someone sitting in a closed-up car in this heat, so I don't take the time to reapply my lip gloss. Instead I get out of the car and nod at her like I'm totally used to driving and it's no big deal.

I walk quickly down the sidewalk, checking my phone for directions to the restaurant. The temperature is still warm, but everyone is talking about the change that's coming. This roller-coaster weather is evidently typical for Texas, especially for October. I pass a white wooden gazebo in the town square. The romantic, old-fashioned structure reminds me of old movies: brass bands playing to picnicking people. That's where the fantasy ends. Instead of a lush lawn of grassy park stretching out around the gazebo, it's crammed in beside a thick, gigantic block of brick that is the Walker County Courthouse.

I think of the courthouse back in Colorado. The victim impact statement. My stomach tightens. I won't think about that now.

I keep walking and I pass a moose. A two-story-high plastic moose, standing on top of the Tri-State Sporting Goods and Archery Shop, with a broken right ear. Looking up at it, I think it has probably been standing guard there, between the Triangle Bowling Alley and Adelaide's Resale Shop, for a long, long time. I pass an assortment of abandoned wedding dresses in the plate glass windows of the resale shop and quickly head toward the bright yellow door of La Ventana. Luis is waiting right inside the door.

"Hi," I say.

He watches me put my keys away in my bag. "You're driving?" he asks, his eyebrows furrowing.

"Just got my license. First outing by myself."

"Congrats," he says, but his expression tells me he understands what a feat this really was.

I nod. "Thanks."

He greets the woman behind the counter in fluent Spanish and they carry on a quick conversation that leaves me understanding only about one word out of four. I might have understood more, but I am busy looking around the small restaurant for anyone who might recognize me.

"I haven't seen you out at the track. Been running lately?" he asks after we're seated by the window.

"No." I glance outside. Anyone walking by can see us sitting here.

The waitress, a dark-haired girl with a yellow heart tattoo on her bare shoulder, slaps the menus on the table and I jump. She asks us if we'd like anything to drink and we both order Cokes.

I look across the table at Luis and my attention shifts. His eyes are so dark brown, I can't see where the pupil ends and the deep color begins. He looks at me and only me. I glance down at the chiseled arm lying across the tabletop. His smooth brown skin. In spite of myself, I want to reach out and touch him. Blair and Mia could be standing directly outside and I wouldn't even notice right now.

The waitress returns with our tall icy glasses of Coke. Then she puts a bowl of tortilla chips on the table along with two bowls of salsa, one red and one green. It's a welcome interruption and gives me enough time to recover.

"Hey," Luis says when the waitress has left. His face lights up as he grins. "My grandmother and Mrs. Annie Florence said to tell you hello."

I can't help but smile back.

"How are they?" I ask.

"They're fine." Luis grabs a chip and dips it in the green salsa. "My dad finally took the delivery van keys away from my grandmother last week after she backed into the next-door neighbors' trash cans. She's not too happy about that."

"What was she delivering?" I'm thinking coffins and bodies.

"Mostly flowers. Now I guess that's one more job I'll need to pick up." He bites into the chip.

"You work a lot."

"After my brother left for college last year, my dad needed the help."

"And you don't miss doing things with your friends?" I ask, and then feel embarrassed because I don't really know if he has any.

"Yeah. Sometimes," he says. "But it was my choice." He takes another bite of a chip, dripping salsa onto the table. "Oops."

I pull a napkin out of the holder in the center of the table and hand it to him. He wipes up the salsa with a grimace.

"My grandmother used to write cheesy messages on napkins and put them in my lunch," he says. "Didn't stop until I finally begged her to in middle school. She thought it was hysterical."

He flips over the napkin in his hand and pretends to read aloud. "'Today is the first day of the rest of your life. Love, *Tu Abuelita*.'"

I laugh. "Your mom didn't pack your lunches?" I ask. I feel a pang, remembering how Mom used to enjoy getting creative with lunches for me and Miranda. Back before the only food she cared about was tomatoes.

Luis's smile vanishes, and I instantly feel bad. "My mom left a few years ago," he replies softly. "Said she couldn't stand living with all the sadness anymore. She took the truck and the dog. Left me and my brother behind."

He glances away and rubs the back of his neck. I don't know what to say. When he looks back at me, he says, "We haven't seen her since."

"Sorry . . ." My voice trails off into silence.

"I don't talk about it much to most people." He shifts his weight; his chair scrapes loudly against the floor.

Trying to be casual, I dip a tortilla chip into the green sauce and take a big bite. The spicy heat grabs me by surprise. I choke out a gasp and frantically reach for my Coke.

Luis laughs as I take a long gulp. "It's got a kick to it."

"No kidding," I pant, waving a hand desperately to fan my tongue.

"Try this one. It's not so hot." He pushes the red sauce in my direction.

I hesitate.

"Trust me," he says.

I take a tentative bite and am relieved that my mouth doesn't burst into flames. It is just right. I take another bite and then another.

"Maybe we'll make a Texas girl out of you yet," Luis says.

"Maybe," I say, after a pause to swallow.

"When do you go back to Colorado?" he asks.

"I'm not sure. Probably in December." My mouth feels really dry all of a sudden and I take another long sip of Coke, glancing around the tiny café. A man sitting at the bright orange countertop is wearing a cowboy hat and suspenders. Boulder seems like another world.

"You're still planning to speak in court?" Luis asks.

"Yes. It's one way I can show people I'm not a monster."

"Why would anyone think that?"

Because without me, Miranda wouldn't have been at the mall that day. She wouldn't have left angry. The car wouldn't have hit her.

"There was a video," I admit after a moment. "People saw us argue that day. It makes me look really . . . bad." I stare down at the chips. "I need to show them how I really felt about Miranda."

"Show who?" Luis asks.

"The people in the courtroom. My followers online. Everyone."

"And *everyone* is important to you?" he asks. I know he's talking about my vlog.

"The funeral home is important to you. You said you were good at it, right?" I don't want to sound defensive, but I know I do.

"Yes," he says.

"I'm good at vlogging. It's not some kind of silly hobby."

"I didn't say it was."

My face feels hot and I feel the anger pushing out my words. "Fashion vloggers get sponsorship deals from major brands. They turn YouTube fame into product deals, magazine spreads, and more traditional journalism gigs as well."

"And that's why you do it?" He waits, patiently.

"Yes," I say, which is true, but it's so much more than that, and I don't even know where to start. I don't want to talk about this. It's obvious he doesn't understand. I pretend to be suddenly fascinated with the menu in front of me. "It doesn't matter," I mumble.

"Hey." He reaches across the table and taps on the top of the menu to get my attention. I look up, meeting his eyes. "I like that you're so bold and opinionated. You don't back down."

"Really?" I'm floored.

Is that how you think of me?

He nods, and his smile switches on to full, blazing wattage. "I wish I were better at it."

"What'll you have?" The waitress is back, fishing a pad of paper out of her pocket and pulling a fake rose from behind her ear. It turns out to be a pen.

Luis orders chiles rellenos, extra hot, and I try to read the menu quickly and refocus. Finally, I give up and just order the chicken tacos, which seem most familiar.

Luis looks at me with raised eyebrows, still waiting, when the waitress leaves. "So have you figured out what you're going to say? In court?"

"The district attorney told my parents the statement should focus on the person who died, who they were, the life they led. That kind of thing," I explain, taking a chip but unable to eat it. "It's our opportunity to tell the judge how all of this has impacted our family."

"That's a lot of pressure." Luis dips a chip in the hot salsa and takes a bite. He waits for me to keep talking, and I do.

"I'm usually good at speaking in front of people. Obviously. I mean, I never get stage fright. But this . . ." I stop and look down at my lap. "This is harder than I thought it would be."

There's a long silence. He doesn't interrupt it.

"My sister and I just . . ." I say softly, tearing at my napkin, "grew apart the last few years."

I am suddenly aware of all the other noise around us — the clink of the glasses being collected from the next table and the man in the cowboy hat speaking on his cell phone.

"So how do you usually prepare to talk to all those people?" Luis asks.

"For the vlog?" I ask, looking up to meet his eyes.

He nods.

"Research, I guess. I try out the makeup. Go to the store. Whatever. Then it comes naturally and I just talk into the camera . . ." My voice trails off and I unfold and refold the yellow cotton napkin in my lap.

"Maybe you should try and think of the court statement the same way," Luis suggests. "Do some research about your sister."

The waitress arrives with our order and we sit silently as she puts the plates in front of us.

"You need anything else?" she asks. I notice for the first time that she's young and pretty, and giving Luis a big smile. I feel a flash of instant jealousy, but Luis doesn't seem to pay her much attention. Instead, he looks across the table at me with raised eyebrows, and I shake my head.

"I think we're good," he tells the waitress.

For a few minutes we both eat without talking. The chicken tacos are delicious, better than any Mexican food I ever had in Colorado.

I work up my nerve, swallow, and say, "Maybe you could help with the research."

"Me?" Luis smiles in surprise. "I didn't know your sister."

"I know, but . . ." Everything that's been rattling around in my head pours out into questions with no pauses in between. "You've seen a lot of people talk about death, right? Memorials and stuff like that? You have, like . . ." I search for a word, and nothing seems right in this situation. "Practice?"

He looks up from his plate. "Sure. I guess so."

Asking for help feels like jumping off a cliff into a free-fall dive. But it is too late to turn back. "How do I start?"

He studies me carefully and then asks, "Have you been to the cemetery yet?"

"No. Why?"

He shrugs. "It's where a lot of people find peace after someone dies. I think of it as a place you can go to deal with anything still needing to be said. Maybe that's where you start."

I think about it. "Can you give me directions?" I ask.

"Your sister is out at the Ferris Family Cemetery. It's way back in the woods off Highway 30. A lot of those roads don't even have names. You have to know where you're going. Why not ask your parents to take you?"

"They have a lot on their minds right now," I mumble, not wanting to explain how my mom doesn't drive much since Miranda's death and my dad is gone all the time. I put the half-eaten taco down on the plate. Silently, I trace a heart shape that's been carved into the wooden tabletop.

"I guess I could draw you a map." Luis holds up his fork, considering a moment before sinking it back into the melted cheese in front of him.

I think driving through the woods while looking at a map would be completely overwhelming. There's no way I could drive miles out of town by myself. I was a nervous wreck just getting here, and it was only a few miles from my house; and I don't want to go alone.

Mostly, I don't want to go alone.

"Can you take me out there?" I ask.

"I thought you were driving now."

"I am, but . . ." I glance up, suddenly hopefully. I can tell he's considering it. "What does it look like? The cemetery."

He eats a few more bites before saying, "It's a pretty place. Sits right on the edge of the Sam Houston National Forest. In the spring, one whole side is covered in bluebonnets."

That sounds nice. Blue was Miranda's favorite color.

"It's old," he continues. "Some of the gravestones go back to the eighteen hundreds. Why did your parents pick that place anyway? It's a long way from Colorado."

"My father's family is all buried there, way back to my grandfather's father."

Luis nods. "There are a lot of families there. You can see the same names repeated over and over on the tombstones."

"I need to see it," I say.

"I have to make a delivery out there later this week." At my expression, he adds, "Flowers. I'm delivering *flowers*."

"Great," I say, feeling like a huge weight has been lifted off my shoulders. "You're delivering flowers, and me."

BEAUTYBASHER.COM

**Board Index*FAQ*News*Chat*Register*Login*

Board Index/Trash a Beauty Vlogger/Beautystarz15

BEAUTYSTARZ15 VIDEO LEAKED

Re: BEAUTYSTARZ15 VIDEO LEAKED

Forever16 wrote: Is it still up? I want to see if it's real.

Re: Re: BEAUTYSTARZ15 VIDEO LEAKED

Raventress wrote: Interesting. They took down the video. I wonder what this will mean for her.

Re: Re: Re: BEAUTYSTARZ15 VIDEO LEAKED

QueenPink wrote: Yep. It's real. Torrey should just talk about it and not ignore it. She's naive to think it will just disappear.

Re: Re: Re: Re: BEAUTYSTARZ15 VIDEO LEAKED

Cheergirl wrote: How can she be so shameless and act so innocent after what she did? I always knew she was a fake little sellout. Fake personality. Fake face. Fake voice. Fake. Fake. Fake.

Re: Re: Re: Re: Re: BEAUTYSTARZ15 VIDEO LEAKED

Heartsticks wrote: I always said she was a horrible little twit. Look how she talked to her poor little sister! Now everyone can see her true colors.

"If you want to start your own channel, be personable! That's the most important thing to remember."

—Torrey Grey, Beautystarz15

CHAPTER FIFTEEN
STONE-COLD NEUTRALS

"I think the purple looks good on him, don't you?" Raylene asks me.

It's Thursday afternoon and she's standing in front of my house. I'm trying to decipher my notes from biology while waiting for Luis to take me to the cemetery, but the breeze on the porch keeps blowing my notebook pages back and forth. The constant flutter of the paper, and Raylene, makes it impossible to concentrate. I could go back inside, but my mom is sitting on the couch in the living room. There will be tons of questions if Luis comes to the door. So I'm stuck outside with Raylene and Stu.

I look down at the cat, who is wearing a new sequined harness.

"He doesn't look so thrilled about it to me."

"I saw this show on TV this weekend where this guy walked his cat everywhere on a leash just like a dog."

"So how did that work for you so far?" I actually already know the answer, since I just watched Raylene try to drag a very angry Stu, spinning and spitting, down the sidewalk on a matching purple sequined leash.

"Very funny," she says sarcastically. "He'll learn. He's just a little stubborn."

"You think?" I stare down at Stu, who stares back up at me. I think he's trying to send me psychic cat signals to say, *Please take that stupid harness off.* I narrow my eyes and send him back a mental message, *Sorry, boy.*

I can tell it's killing Raylene to not know what I'm doing hanging around outside on the porch, but the last thing I want is for her to be here when Luis pulls up. She needs to leave and take that cat with her. So far I haven't come up with a plan to make that happen.

"I see you eating lunch at Blair's table every day now. You guys look pretty close," Raylene announces as she sits down beside me on the steps. She's wearing a red tank top with the word *Juicy* spelled out in rhinestones across the front. She is also wearing blue-jean cutoffs and flip-flops. "I try to get her to just say hello for the last two years and in four weeks you're sitting at her lunch table with all her minions. How did you do it?"

"Popular is as popular does. It's all about building the buzz," I say, like I'm talking to my viewers on my vlog. The plan for popularity is moving along slowly, but it's working. Every day, I'm getting just a little bit closer to Blair's inner circle. I don't wait to be asked to sit at her table anymore.

"And that's exactly why I'm trying out for twirling. I'm building the buzzzzzz." Raylene stretches out the *Z* sound into at least three syllables. She crosses one bare leg over the top of the other and pulls the October issue of *Glamour* magazine out of her hobo bag. I try to ignore the foot swinging in and out of my peripheral vision, the mingled smell of several different brands of perfume coming from the magazine, and the blinged-out cat sitting at my feet.

"By the way, do you think this color makes my legs look golden brown?" she asks.

I looked at her bright pink toes. "I guess so."

"Remember your post about pedicures last May? When you said baby pink was the best color to go with a tan?"

"Yes," I say, surprised she remembers.

"Well, this is as close to Poppin' Pink — the one you showed — as I could find." She stretches one leg out in front of her and we both stare at it for a few minutes in silence. Then, in typical Raylene fashion, she changes the subject. "Have you been to Jilly's yet?"

"No," I say, but I know it's where all the popular kids hang out after school. So far Blair hasn't asked me, but she will. Baby steps with lots of smiles and compliments. I'll get there. "I've been really busy."

"Uh-huh," Raylene says, like she doesn't believe me. Then she turns a page in the magazine, pries open yet another perfume ad from an insert, and rubs the paper on her inner elbow. She pauses a moment, takes a big sniff of her arm, and then begins flipping pages again. "Did you know Ross Adams plays the drums, which everyone knows is the coolest instrument possible to play if you're in band?"

Raylene's train of thought is as hard to follow as always. I turn the page of my biology notes and frown like I'm concentrating really hard.

Go home, Raylene. Go home, Raylene.

"I thought he played football," I say, and then mentally kick myself, because that's just going to encourage the conversation.

"He plays that, too. Wide receiver."

I turn a page in my biology notebook and slide it under one leg to try and keep it from blowing back again. "Didn't know he was so multitalented."

"Oh, Ross is *really* good at football. Like, varsity-as-a-sophomore kind of good."

I glance over. Sounds like somebody has a crush on Ross. "Yeah. I saw him practicing."

"Our team probably would have been in the playoffs next year if Luis hadn't quit. It threw the whole team off."

"Luis?"

My heart jumps.

Luis Rivera?

"You didn't know?" Raylene says, still intent on the magazine. "He and Ross were an amazing duo until Luis just walked away from it all."

No, I didn't know Luis played football. Or that he and Ross used to be friends.

"What happened?" I ask, still trying to process this new information.

"Not sure," Raylene says, rubbing on more perfume

samples. "By the way, I need a favor. You know that my twirling solo competition is next weekend, right?"

"No," I say, looking up the street to see if Luis is coming. I'm starting to actually follow Raylene's constantly changing topics. It scares me a little.

"Alysia Warwick singed her arm on a flaming baton last week, and that puts her out of the competition. And you know who that moves right into one of the top three spots?"

"No," I say.

"Me, silly!" Raylene grins and nudges me. "So it's going to be down in Conroe next weekend, and I need to go down early to get in line and practice and everything. You understand, right?"

"No." I glance down at my watch. Luis should be here any minute.

Go home, Raylene. Go home, Raylene.

"Well, my parents are going to go, of course, and we both know I can't leave Stu alone all weekend with his separation-anxiety issues and all, so . . ."

"NO," I say louder. Now I know where this is going. "I am not cat-sitting, Raylene."

"He just likes to be around people," Raylene says.

I sigh.

"It's just for the weekend," Raylene continues pleadingly, "and Stu really LOVES you. I wouldn't leave him with just anyone."

Stu sits at my feet and stares at me with green unblinking eyes.

"I can't take care of the cat. I have plans," I say to both of them.

"You have *plans*?" Raylene asks.

Uh-oh. Now I am on dangerous ground. My quick little white lie is going to need some creative detail.

"So what are you going to wear to the competition?" I ask, trying to change the subject. It's too late.

"You DO have plans. What kind of plans?" Raylene's eyes narrow in interest.

"Nothing much. No big deal." As the words are coming out of my mouth, I'm trying to frantically think of something.

"Girrrrlllllllllllll! And you weren't going to TELL me?" She yells so loudly I jump. "Big date? With who? Luis?"

"Why would you say that?" I snap. Why would Raylene even think this was a possibility?

Raylene smiles. "I saw you guys jogging together last week. I don't care what Blair says about him. He's a . . . dor . . . a . . . ble!" She draws out the word admiringly. "All those muscles. And you guys probably have a lot to talk about."

"Like dead people?" I ask sarcastically.

"Okay. Okay. Obviously someone is in a bad mood this afternoon." She slides off my porch step, leaving behind a cloud of perfume and taking the magazine with her.

She is right. I'm not in a talking mood. I have too many things tumbling around inside my sleep-deprived brain.

"But you're still going to take care of Stu, right?" Raylene calls out from the end of the driveway.

"My dad is going out of town that weekend, so I'll have to ask my mom," I say, thinking that this is my way out. I'll tell Raylene that Mom said no. I lean over to put away my biology notes, trying to escape her curious eyes.

"Your mom already said yes. I talked to her after school."

My shoulders slump down in surrender. Raylene is exhausting.

"Fine. I'll do it," I say in a small voice. I give up.

"Great. I'll bring you a big bag of Mr. Purrfect and his leash when I drop him off next Saturday." Point, Raylene.

Stu jumps up on my lap, turns around once, and then curls into a massive ball of fur and purple glitter. Within seconds, his eyes close to slits and I hear the satisfied rumble of his purr. I am now officially a cat-sitter. Point, Stu.

"Come back and get this cat," I call out.

Raylene retrieves Stu and pulls him across the street on his leash just as the black van pulls up to the curb with the lettering RIVERA FUNERAL HOME on the side panel. Great. I'm going to a hidden cemetery in a funeral parlor van.

Luckily, no one else seems to be watching except for Raylene and a very grumpy Stu.

Luis rolls down the window as I come around the front of the van. "Something wrong?" he asks.

"No," I say, opening the passenger side and sliding in. "Let's go."

I wave a quick good-bye to a gaping Raylene, and close the van door firmly behind me. There will definitely be questions when I get back, but I'll deal with that later.

"Hey." Luis nods at me and I give him a quick smile. "Sorry I'm a little late."

"No problem." I think back to Raylene's surprising bit of information about Luis.

He played football? With Ross? So he wasn't always the outcast from Blair's society?

We turn left and head out on Highway 30. The cemetery is about ten miles outside of town, so there is plenty of time to talk. Whether I want to or not. I glance sideways at Luis's profile.

"So you used to play football?" I ask casually, as though it's no big deal.

"Yes," he says, but he doesn't elaborate and there is no sign of that face-changing grin.

I push a little harder, curious. "Why did you stop?"

He looks over at me, then back to the road. "It took up too much time. I needed to work."

Then he reaches out and clicks on the radio, effectively cutting off my questions with the violins of a country-western song. I want to ask him more, but the subject is obviously closed.

So I pull out my phone. There are two more texts from Zoe and a missed call. I ignore it. The gossip board is still going crazy with comments about the video even though it's not even up anymore. Each typed sentence holds up or down a thumb like a Roman arena of opinions. The lions are pacing outside the gates, slashing through the monitor with razor-sharp opinions.

I'm not who you think I am.

Or maybe I am.

I feel a rush of anger and make myself look away from the screen. "Thank you for doing this," I say to Luis.

He glances sideways at me again, then back ahead. "You're welcome."

There is a long silence after that. I put my phone away in my pocket and stare straight ahead at the highway stretching out into the forest on either side.

"What happened to him?" he finally asks.

"Who?" I glance over.

"The man who killed your sister."

I look back out the front window at the pine trees flashing by. "He's in prison in Colorado. There was a deal. He pled guilty and is going to be sentenced in December."

"And that's when you'll make this statement?"

"Yeah," I say.

We drive for a few more minutes in silence until Luis speaks again. "Tell me more about your sister."

"What do you want to know?"

"Whatever you feel like telling me."

I think about my response for a minute. "She had this really quirky sense of humor. For her birthday, she always tried to ask for something weird. The stranger and harder to find, the better. Shopping was always my thing and she was always trying to stump me. It was like a tradition."

He smiles, but doesn't say anything. I keep talking.

"I don't remember how it started. Last year, she wanted socks with pictures of socks on them."

He laughs.

"She thought the idea of those socks was hysterically funny. Socks with socks. She collapsed with giggles every time she said the phrase."

Miranda had a great laugh. It was infectious. It was so silly, but the memory makes me smile.

When she was younger, she and Mom used to giggle hysterically over stupid jokes like *Why did the chicken cross the playground? To get to the other slide.* They looked so much alike, with blond curls and big blue eyes, and when they were together they even acted alike — laughing at the same jokes and singing out loud to the same songs on the radio.

"Did she get them?" Luis asks.

"What?" I blink away the memory of my mom and Miranda singing "Baby Beluga" at the top of their lungs.

"Did she ever get the socks with socks?"

"No. Surprisingly, they're hard to find. I was going to try again this year. . . ." My voice trails off and we both think about why it wouldn't matter now.

I take a lot of pride in giving perfect gifts. And Miranda's gift challenges were the only times she actually appreciated my talent. On birthdays and Christmas, it was okay for me to be the master shopper. She didn't turn up her nose at how much effort I spent on shopping. I could always eventually find the right thing for each individual.

Things. Like the things in my closet.

Luis turns off the two-lane highway onto a gravel path that leads back into the woods. A clearing comes into view and I realize I'm holding my breath. He pulls up beside a low iron fence and turns off the van.

The oak trees are big and old, with many limbs already bare from the first cool weather of fall. Gray moss hangs from low-lying branches and blows softly in the wind. It's quiet. There's a small gate, and beyond are white headstones sticking out randomly from the cover of brown and yellow leaves on the ground.

"Her grave is near the back. I'll show you when you're ready."

I let my breath out in a long sigh. "I'm ready," I say, raising my chin.

I slide out of the van and slam the door shut. We walk slowly toward the gate, the only sound the crunch of the leaves beneath our feet. On the far side of the perfectly maintained little clearing, the forest takes over again. The trunks of pine trees are tightly packed into a thick line against the back fence, every possible ground space between them filled with vines.

"Do you want me to go with you?" Luis asks quietly, holding open the gate.

"No."

"Walk straight through the middle. The newer graves are in the back. It's right under that big oak back there." He points, and I nod weakly. Ropes of vines drape from the treetops in junglelike profusion, but inside the tiny clearing, the trees are old and solitary, spaced out among the gravestones to provide shade. "I've got some arrangements to put out."

There are no other people here now, but the left behind have obviously been here. Their flowers and remembrances are scattered throughout. The only sign of life is a squirrel that makes a quick retreat with a pecan sticking out of one side of its mouth.

I walk carefully back through the stones, trying not to step directly on a grave. The stones are old, some cracked and crumbling, with dates from the eighteen hundreds. One has a tiny lamb on it with a missing ear. Another has a dove etched into the granite with two miniature stones on either side. I should feel scared, but I only feel the profound quiet. I glance at the dates of the three headstones in front of me. All the same last name. A mother and her two children? What terrible thing happened to them in 1938? I can't stop and wonder. There are newer markings now, less crumbled stone and more polished granite. All have stories. Lives lived and people left behind to grieve.

Without warning, the question from Miranda's game of hide-and-seek breathes through my mind. *You're not coming to find me, are you?*

But I am.

I keep walking, heading directly toward the big tree Luis pointed out. The tombstones get even more modern, the dates more current. Some even have photographs etched into the stone. One is covered in pictures of cats and has the family name, Rattenborg, engraved on top. I glance at the date. She died last year.

And then I'm there. The grass hasn't grown over the dirt yet. The name on the stone is stark and cold — *Miranda Jo Grey*. And underneath, the date of her birth and her death, and the words *Gone but not forgotten*.

"When the moon shines bright, your fears will be few . . ." I whisper softly, my finger tracing the outline of the words, "and only sweet dreams will come to you."

The guilt feels like a kick to my stomach. But, then, it's always been there, waiting on the edges of my mind and haunting my dreams.

If only I didn't make you go to the mall. If only I wasn't mean to you. If only I stopped you. If only I apologized. If only . . .

I drop to my knees in front of the tombstone. The etched name is cold under my fingers. I trace it once, and then again. All I feel is stone. The wind blows gently at the moss. The silence is absolute. There is no response. No giggles. No chatter. No arguing. Nothing. How could there be nothing? How could she be nothing?

I struggle to my feet, wiping the dirt off my hands. There's a concrete bench and I sit down, pulling my jacket in a little tighter to my body even though it's not cold. The brown barren patch of earth looks so lonely. I try to imagine it covered with an altar full of *ofrendas* and bright yellow flowers. It's comforting somehow.

"Are you okay?" Luis is standing in front of me.

"I was just thinking."

"Well, now you don't have to think. You can talk."

"Maybe it'd be easier if you were filming me," I say casually, but I might actually mean it, and that makes me feel even worse.

"Action," he says with a small smile, then squats down in front of me and reaches for my hands. He holds them lightly in his and waits. I don't pull my hands free. I don't want to.

"Luis?" I say, and he looks at me expectantly. "What do you think happens when you die?" Here in this place, I have to ask.

"No one knows the answer to that for sure." He holds my gaze solemnly. "But being around death all my life, I have some ideas on the subject."

"Like what?" I listen, fascinated.

"What if it wasn't a bad thing? Dying."

"But it is. A bad thing, I mean."

"It's a bad thing for you. For everyone left behind. Because you miss them."

He looks at me for a reaction, but I am not sure what to say.

"Think of it this way. Say someone was walking through this really big mud pile and there were, like, snakes everywhere and lots of dirty, slimy water and she felt sick and tired and was really, really struggling through that water and it was dark everywhere."

"So you're saying the world is like that?"

"Just stay with me for a minute. So you see her struggling to walk through all that mud and you know you could help. You could take her to a place where it would be warm and light and she'd feel great, but she'd have to leave the muddy, yucky place behind. Would you do it?"

"Of course," I say. "And maybe I could believe that for sick people who die or old people, but what about kids?"

We both know who I am talking about.

"It's sort of the same kind of thing," he says.

"So everybody here on earth is just waiting to go to the big party in the sky?" I don't mean to sound so sarcastic, but I'm not buying it. "My sister was a happy kid and she loved life. She wasn't sitting around suffering, waiting for something better."

"All I'm saying is maybe we just don't know any better than *here*." Luis stares off into space in an unfocused way, and the look on his face is so still I am afraid to say a word.

I try to digest this idea.

"This better place — is it heaven?"

"I'm not sure what to call it. I just think it exists."

"So you believe in God, too?" I ask.

"Yeah. I do," he said. "You?"

"I don't know anymore."

"That's okay." He looks like he means it. "But if some kind of afterlife exists, then dying wouldn't be bad at all, right?"

I still can't agree with him, but I will think about what he said. The next question rattles around inside my head until I finally blurt it out. "Do you think sometimes people stay around . . . you know . . . afterward?"

"I think there could be reasons sometimes for them to stay." Luis looks at me, almost curiously. "It's a very small space between the living and the dead. Why wouldn't there be some overlap?"

"Yeah. Maybe." I look down at the ground, kicking at the leaves with the tip of my shoe, before I look back up to meet his eyes. "I just want proof."

"There's a lot of stuff we believe without proof." His dark eyes become thoughtful. "Think about the Internet. We all know it's out there. We use it every day, but have you ever seen it?"

"No," I say slowly. "But even if you can't see it, there is proof the Internet exists."

Like my vlog. All the people out there, listening to me. Responding to me.

"I've seen lots of things I can't explain," Luis says quietly. "I don't know if it's proof or not. Doors opening when no one was there. Shadows. Voices."

"It doesn't bother you? Scare you?" Thinking about ghosts makes me shiver.

"It's just part of my life, I guess." Luis sits down beside me on the bench and slips an arm around my shoulders, pulling me into him. It throws me off balance, but only for a minute. I feel the warmth of his broad chest against my side and slowly melt down into him. It feels too good to pull away.

"How do you know all this?" I ask.

"I hear a lot of sermons from a lot of different ministers. All those funerals."

I think about that for a moment. It makes sense.

"You are good at comforting people," I say.

We sit like that for a while, beside Miranda's grave, not talking. The quiet surrounding us, the wind soft on our faces. I think about the cemetery in Luis's grandmother's town in Mexico, where the *angelitos* visit the living at midnight. This could be such a place.

"Thanks for bringing me," I say finally.

"I didn't have much of a choice. You're pretty convincing when you set your mind to something."

I laugh. The squirrel scampers back out through the leaves, across the graves, digging around for another nut. A brown bushy piece of life among all the death. We watch it in silence.

"It must have been tough coming here, but you did it. You're stronger than you look."

But how I look is what I'm good at.

I change the subject, uncomfortable with the compliment. "Have you ever spent the night out here before?" I ask, looking toward the thicket of woods surrounding us.

He doesn't ask why I want to know. He only nods. "The summer after my mom left, I was at this camp where they had this solo thing. They put you out in those woods." He points toward the fence and the trees. "All you have is a tarp, some food, water, and a sleeping bag. You stay there for twelve hours by yourself."

"Why?" I ask, because it just sounds crazy.

"It's supposed to help you get in touch with your feelings and stuff like that." He grins.

"What's out there?" I ask.

"Tons of mosquitoes, of course."

"Of course."

"Big cottonmouth snakes that curl up in the hollows of pine trees and open their mouths in wide screams when you walk past them." He opens his mouth to demonstrate. "That's in the daytime. When you can see them."

I cringe at the thought of what happens at night when you can't.

"And, of course, there are feral hogs. They run wild all over these woods and they are meeeean." He draws the last word out into about five syllables for emphasis. "You do not want to run into one of those out there."

He's right. I don't.

"After it gets dark, you can hear these big, clumsy armadillos crashing through the underbrush like huge half-blind tanks."

"I don't think we have armadillos in Colorado."

"They look like tiny dinosaurs. They're harmless, but they're oblivious to everything."

"Good to know," I say, but I'm thinking more about the snakes and wild hogs than the armadillos. Luis leans forward to put both palms down on his knees, his bicep stretching the arm of his white T-shirt. Not that I notice. "It sounds horrible."

He shrugs. "It wasn't that bad. Even though I felt alone, I wasn't really. The camp counselors were only a whistle blow away."

"So what was the point?"

"I guess it's about having time to think — without any distractions. Something about being truly alone, with all the sounds and darkness, helps you figure some things out."

"What if you realize you don't like your own company? It might make for a really long night. . . ." My voice trails off to a whisper.

He tilts his head and looks over at me. "Why do you ask?"

"I was just thinking about *el Día de los Muertos* and how people spend all night in the graveyard."

"In Mexico, there'd be plenty of people to keep you company. Out here, it'd just be you and the armadillos," he says.

And snakes.

"But you survived," I point out. "And all that time in the woods by yourself was a good thing?"

He considers for a moment. "For me it was. There was something about just sitting outside in the dark all alone. Makes you face your demons, you know?"

"I guess." I know all about demons and the dark, but I'm not sure I want to face either one.

"The secret to being a real star is commitment."

—Torrey Grey, Beautystarz15

CHAPTER SIXTEEN
PICTURE-PERFECT MAKEUP TUTORIAL

When I get home from the cemetery, I see my dad mowing the lawn. I wave on my way inside, grateful that I won't have to answer questions about Luis or the funeral home van right now.

I find my mom in her bedroom, sitting on the floor in front of her dresser. Photographs of a family that used to have four people are scattered around her outstretched legs. I sit down on the side of the bed.

"Remember this one?" She holds up a photograph, her hand trembling. I know it well. It used to sit in a frame on top of our entertainment center in Colorado.

"Yes," I say. It was my thirteenth birthday and we hiked Torreys Peak, my namesake, for the first time as a family. It was a crisp fall day and the aspens were bright yellow against the blue Colorado sky. Miranda didn't want to go all the way to the top, so we stopped halfway. I begged my dad to keep going with me, but he said we weren't going to split up. He asked another hiker to snap a picture of us. In the photo, I'm scowling and looking away from the camera. My mom is smiling, brushing Miranda's wild curls back from her face with one hand, and my dad has his arms around all of us in a big bear hug.

"It was a good day," Mom says, pressing the photo to her chest. Her breathing is so quiet. I'm afraid she is crying, but when I make myself look, she isn't.

She picks up another photo off the floor and holds it out toward me. It was our Christmas-card picture from last year. Miranda is in red and I'm in green — smiling brightly in front of a big fake photo-studio Christmas tree.

One would never guess that my sister and I were always arguing, out of the frame. Meanwhile, everything else in my life at that moment was coming into perfect, sharp focus. My vlog was featured on TeenVogue.com and I was named one of the top ten teen beauty vloggers to watch. Page views and followers were skyrocketing. I shared my possessions and opinions freely with the world. I started spending more time watching YouTube than television. Every day I received messages from girls all over the world thanking me for being their inspiration. My extended social group copied my looks and retweeted my words. None of that is visible in this standard photo.

"Remember how she used to lie under the Christmas tree and count the seconds between each blink of the lights?" my mom asks.

I nod. At the time I thought it was incredibly annoying. Now I would give anything to see Miranda under the Christmas tree. Or anywhere else.

Mom slowly opens her fingers and the picture falls back onto the scattered pile of frozen moments in time. I slide off the end of the bed and join her on the floor, reaching out for her empty hand. It feels cold and dry.

"I think about her all the time. If I could just talk to her," Mom says. Her voice sounds hoarse and sleepy. "But I can't even talk *about* her."

It's an astonishing echo of my words to Luis earlier. Evidently neither Mom nor I can share the pain out loud. But we are here. Surrounded by the images of our used-to-be life and bound together in the silent intensity of grief.

"It just takes time." I say what everyone says, but my throat hurts and I can hardly force the words out. The truth is I don't know what it will take to put our world together again.

"I don't want to do it anymore," Mom mumbles, almost to herself. Almost like she's forgotten I'm here.

I feel a sharp understanding of what she's saying, but I won't accept it. I can't lose anyone else. "You don't mean that," I say.

"I wanted to be really brave at this. I wanted to be noble and courageous and strong." Tears well up in her eyes and slowly leak down her cheeks. "But I don't feel brave or courageous or strong. I just feel broken."

"You can't give up, Mom." The tears are running down my cheeks, too. The pain so deep in my chest, I can't breathe. *I'm still here. I need you.*

"I'm not like you and your dad," she replies. "You both

always figure out what to do next." She leans against me. "I don't know what to do next."

She puts her head in my lap and I brush her hair back from her face. She looks so different now. Her features changed forever, collapsing into the terrible lines of unrecognizable pain, in the hospital corridor when she collapsed into my dad's arms at the news Miranda would never wake up.

I'm sorry, Mom. So sorry.

"I don't know what to do," I murmur out loud, but I'm not sure she even hears me. Her eyes close and I look down at her still, sad face. Sometimes watching my mom with Miranda made me feel unimportant. Unnecessary. Unchosen. I was the changeling, with my dark hair and tall lanky body, who no one thought was related to the rest of the family. The dark, moody teenager. I just wanted to be left alone with all my Internet friends. "Can you just leave me alone, Miranda?" I always said. "Mom, tell Miranda to leave me alone."

I don't want to be alone.

"Please, Mom. I need you here," I whisper.

We stay like that for a long time without saying anything until she finally opens her eyes and looks up at me. It seems that, finally, she has heard me. She knows that I still need her. She still has another daughter.

Somewhere in this searing, shared pain, I realize that my mom and I are more alike than I knew.

"I love you, Torrey," she mumbles tiredly.

"I know, Mom."

Later in my room, I'm still thinking about my mom. My phone buzzes and I answer without even looking, instantly regretting it.

"Hey," Zoe says. "I'm surprised you picked up."

My heart stops. I don't say anything.

"Please don't hang up."

"What do you want?" I manage to ask. It's so strange to hear her familiar voice after all this time.

"I'm so sorry, Torrey. It totally got out of hand. Please believe me. It was a stupid mistake." The words pour out of her in a torrent.

"Was Cody a mistake, too?" I can't help but ask, sitting up on my bed.

"Yes. Everything. Even that." Zoe doesn't even deny it. "I just missed you. We both did. I thought it would be like hanging out with you somehow."

"That's the stupidest thing I've ever heard." I'm so angry, my hand is shaking and the phone rattles against my ear.

"I know. I know. We're not going out anymore. It's over." She's crying now, and I feel my throat close. "You were the only thing we had in common."

"I don't know what you want me to say."

"Say you forgive me."

I listen to her sobbing, and finally I say, "I can't do that right now."

"Then say you'll at least think about it," she pleads. Begging isn't like her.

"I'll think about it," I say, and end the call.

Much later, when I've calmed down from talking to Zoe, I pull out the backpack and pile of things from my closet. I place each item separately on the bed, spread out like the photos on Mom's floor. They look random and disconnected lying on the bedspread.

This is what a life was made of.

I pick up Miranda's sketchbook page of Sensational Sister. My finger traces the outline of the drawing. I fold it up and put it back on the bed.

What do I say?

I close my eyes and try to imagine speaking in the courtroom, but all I can think about is my mom's head in my lap and the sadness in her face.

Just pack it all up. Hide it away again.

I fold the baby blanket and slide it down into the backpack, surprised when my fingers touch something at the bottom. I turn the bag over and shake it until something falls out. The moonstone bracelet lies uncovered on the bed in front of me. There is no sparkle — no glimmer of moonlight or magic. I pick it up off the sheets and hold it carefully in my hand. Miranda kept it all those years. Even when we screamed at each other and argued. This bracelet was in her backpack all the time.

Like it meant something to her.

A tightness squeezes at my chest. I just want to talk to her. I'd sit by her grave all night, just like they do in Mexico, waiting for her to return. I would say I was sorry and I'd give her the bracelet. Then she'd be okay. Wherever she was.

"Use your friends as your target audience. Ask them what they'd like to see." —**Torrey Grey, Beautystarz15**

CHAPTER SEVENTEEN

BOLD, GUTSY LOOKS TO MAKE YOU THE CENTER OF ATTENTION

Monday afternoon in Spanish class, my phone buzzes. At first I think it's Zoe calling again, and I feel a weird mix of dread and anticipation. But then I see it's a text from a number I don't recognize. *Meet us at Jilly's after school.* I assume it's from Blair because I gave her my number at lunch last week. I was so excited she wanted it, I totally forgot to ask for hers.

When Mrs. Garcia isn't looking, I text back quickly: *K.* Then I spend the rest of class smiling to myself. Evidently I've graduated from lunchtime buddy to after-school buddy. It's definitely progress.

Jilly's is a block from the school and an easy walk. A girl in a vintage sundress with an eyebrow piercing takes my order for a skim latte. While I wait, I check out the rest of the café. It's a narrow space with lime-green walls, wooden tables, and brightly painted mismatched chairs. On one wall is a big chalkboard with blocky red letters that say EXPRESSO

YOURSELF. The rest of the decor is all flyers for local bands and fall community events.

Even with my limited experience at the new school, I recognize most of the crowd. There's the tall girl from my third-period algebra class with the pink streak at her temple. She is wearing a Hello Kitty T-shirt and has a big blue ring pierced through her lip. Ross is here, too. He's wearing a green baseball hat and is over by the window drinking an iced coffee and reading a book. Only he's holding the book like it's a prop in a play, his eyes darting up every time a girl walks by. I haven't seen him turn the page once.

I'm taking my latte off the counter when Mia appears, grabbing my arm and pulling me to a table by the far wall.

"We always sit back here," she says, settling in and then motioning to the chair across from her.

I sit where she points. "Where are Emily and Blair?" I ask, surprised neither are in sight. Mia is never alone.

"They're around somewhere." She shrugs.

That makes me more than a little nervous. "They're coming, right?"

"They're just running late. Besides, this gives us some time to get to know each other better." She leans toward me. "After all, you're the focus of all the conversation right now. The star attraction."

I'm not sure I want to get to know Mia better. Especially not with the way she's looking at me right now. Her stare is intense and cold. I force myself to not look away. Two can play this game.

"What do you want to know?" I ask.

"You aren't fooling me," she says. "You come in with all your perfect hair and your perfect clothes. Just because you look perfect, doesn't mean you are."

Her threatening tone makes me nervous, but I hope I don't show it. "Look, Mia. I never said I was perfect." I laugh a little bit, throwing my hands up to ward off her bitterness.

It doesn't work. "You don't have to say it," she replies coolly. "You *act* it. And that's all it is. An act."

Mia's right. I'm not perfect. Far from it. I start talking fast, trying to calm her down. "Look, Mia. I don't want to upset you. You've obviously got tons of friends here and I'm not trying to take your place."

"Did you know the student body votes on cheerleaders here? It's a complete popularity contest."

I shake my head, wondering if she's changed the subject. I'm confused. "And you're a cheerleader, so you must be super popular," I tell her.

"Blair got me that vote. I'm a cheerleader because of her. She's the one who made people stop calling me 'pizza face' in the fifth grade. She talked Jason Edler into going out with me in the seventh grade. I'm *everything* because of Blair," Mia says, her face twisted with anger.

"You're Blair's best friend," I say. Then I hear myself switch into my beauty-vlogger voice. Perky and exaggerated. "And you're soooo cute. Adorable, really. And THAT'S why you're a cheerleader. It isn't just about Blair. It's about who *you* are."

This tactic seems to work for a moment. Mia blinks, then takes a sip of her chai. When she continues, her voice is softer. "Blair's at the top of the social stratosphere here and she knows it. She can afford to like the charity cases. It makes her look even better."

I pick up my latte, but I don't take a drink.

"And right now," Mia goes on, "you're Blair Cunningham's favorite pity party."

Jealousy does not look pretty, I think. I feel embarrassed for Mia. Her attitude makes her look desperate. Weak.

But I can't help wondering if part of what she's saying is true. If Blair *will* eventually kick me to the curb. Does she know what everyone's saying about me online and simply doesn't care? Or will she be mortified to be seen with me when she finds out? Even worse, she might love the fact that I'm a target and she can rush in to be the savior.

"I'm not trying to take your place," I say to Mia.

"You think she pities *me*?" Mia practically spits out the words. I glance around to see if anyone notices her raised voice.

"I didn't say that."

"Blair may think you're the next best thing, but you know what she's not good at?" Mia asks.

I wait, because I'm sure she's going to tell me no matter what I say, the full cup of coffee growing cold in my cupped hands.

"Competition," Mia says.

"You think I'm trying to compete with Blair?" My voice is rising, but I can't stop now I've started. I glance over to see Ross and the theater girl staring curiously in our direction. I struggle to lower my voice. "For what? Queen of the school?"

"You and Blair are just alike. Both of you need to be the star. And Blair doesn't like to be invisible."

Nobody does.

A commotion at the door is a welcome distraction. Emily and Raylene burst into the café, busy as hummingbirds around a bird feeder. Fighting for position, and in constant fluttery motion. The bird feeder, and the object of their adoration, is Blair.

Blair waves in our general direction. Then she and her hummingbirds flutter over to talk to Ross, giving me enough time to regain my composure. Raylene gives me a quick thumbs-up sign from behind Blair's back, and I wonder how she became a member of this little group. It's definitely a step up in social status.

Mia must have wondered the same thing because the minute they all land at our table, she asks, "What's she doing here?"

I'm just happy to have anything interrupt our conversation, but my hands still tremble with anger. I tuck them under my legs so no one can see.

"She was outside," Emily says. "She followed us in here."

That's a horrible thing to say right in front of her, but Raylene doesn't seem to notice. She just nods like her head is going to fall off. I wish I could tell her to relax, to not look so eager.

"I wanted to tell you all about my Halloween party," Raylene says to Emily and Blair.

Emily makes an exaggerated yawn. "Yeah. It's fascinating," she says.

I feel my face heat up. This is painful.

"It's going to be a blast," Raylene continues. If she can pick up on the girls' disinterest, she's not showing it. "A week from this Friday. Halloween night. You're all coming, right?"

"Not sure," Blair says. "Might be busy."

Mia snorts, and I know I can't be here a second longer.

"Let me out," I mumble. I push against Emily. "I have to go to the bathroom."

"I'll go with you," Raylene calls out behind me.

"Whatever." I head toward the back hallway, hoping I'm going in the right direction. I choose the door with the picture of a poodle wearing a dress instead of the one with a bulldog wearing overalls.

"Do you really think they'll come to my party?" Raylene asks before the door even swings shut behind her.

Are you kidding? "I don't know," I say.

I look into the mirror over the sink, then fumble in my bag for lip gloss. My eyes look bluer than usual in the bright bathroom light. I've never noticed it before, but I really do look like Miranda. Or rather, she looked like me. I try to focus on the part of her that is there in my reflection. I can almost see another face now, floating over the top of mine.

"You could ask them," Raylene says.

"What?"

"Ask them if they will come to my party. They'll do it if you ask them."

She obviously didn't overhear my conversation with Mia. I'm not nearly as popular as she thinks. I mumble something on the way out the door that she's supposed to think is a yes.

"Wait," Raylene calls out behind me as I walk back out to the crowded café. "You're going to do it, right?"

I go back to the table. When I see Mia again, she gives me a fake smile and I realize that yes, I will accept Raylene's challenge. Blair and friends will be at her party. I'll need a plan, of course, but I will do it somehow.

"Hey, Luis," the counter girl says. "What'll it be?"

I freeze, then look over to see Luis ordering a double-shot Americano at the counter. I must have been in the bathroom when he came in. He doesn't glance in our direction.

"I can't believe it," Blair says, wrinkling her nose. "What's he doing here?"

"What's the deal with you and Luis?" I blurt out, no longer caring about how the question might sound.

Mia turns to me. "Blair and Frankenstein used to go out. Until he decided he liked dead people better than her."

I'm stunned. Speechless. *Blair and Luis?* I must make some kind of noise, because Emily looks over at me with eyes narrowed.

"I — I thought she hated him," I stammer, hoping the shock isn't showing on my face.

"She does now," Emily says.

I glance back toward the counter. Luis pays for his drink and leaves. I guess he knows he's not welcome at a place like Jilly's.

"You know he's weird, right?" Blair asks. She's watching me closely. I try to keep my expression neutral.

Why didn't he tell me? And then I think, why *would* he tell me? It's not like we're dating or anything. It's not like he *likes* me. But then I realize with a sinking feeling that I want him to like me, and that's not a good thing. Especially in present company.

"I guess I have a lot to learn about everyone here." I laugh, trying to make a joke of it. To get Blair off the subject. She doesn't go easily.

"Stay away from him," she says, standing up from the table. Immediately Mia and Emily follow her lead, gathering up purses and book bags.

"Where are you guys going?" Raylene asks.

"We're leaving," Emily says.

"It's boring," Mia says, and looks pointedly at me.

"Hey . . ." I start to say something else, but the whole entourage is already heading toward the door.

"Don't forget about my Halloween party," Raylene calls as the door swings shut behind them.

"What party? Did I hear something about a party?" Ross calls out from his table, putting down his book. Raylene happily trots over to fill him in on all the details. I'm left sitting alone.

So much for my first visit to Jilly's. It's obvious Mia hates my guts and is sure to be whispering her snarky opinions right into Blair's ear. Even if I could get them to go to Raylene's party, it would be a disaster. If only Raylene didn't want it so badly. On top of all that, Luis has this past with Blair I knew nothing about. And that bothers me most of all.

I might as well go home.

As I leave, I can hear Raylene telling Ross, "You don't have to dress up, but I'm coming as a black cat."

I walk outside with my head down, digging around in my purse for my keys. The crack in the sidewalk catches the pointed toe of my Steve Madden pump, and I stumble, steadying myself on a lamppost.

"Whoa, girl." Luis is standing at the curb, coffee in one hand. "You better watch where you're going."

I look around to make sure Blair is long gone, and then say, "For my next trick, I'll do a double somersault dismount."

"You never cease to amaze me." He leans against the black van behind him, clapping his hands together slowly.

"Thanks." I give a little bow, but I don't smile. I'm mad at him even though I know it doesn't make any sense.

What about Blair? Did she amaze you?

I keep walking down the sidewalk. With a few quick strides he's beside me.

"You weren't at Jilly's long," he says, sliding into step beside me.

I didn't realize he even knew I was in there. "Were you watching me?" I glare at him.

His smile starts with a crinkle at the side of his dark eyes and then spreads to his mouth. I look at his mouth and then back up to his eyes, swallowing hard, and his grin gets even bigger.

Is that the way you looked at Blair?

"Nope. Just hanging out waiting for Mrs. Johnson to finish a flower arrangement." He motions to a sign on a store window next door that says KAREN'S FLOWERS. "So Jilly's wasn't all it's cracked up to be?"

"It was okay." What do I say? *I found out about you and Blair.* "I have to do my homework," I say instead.

He puts his hand on my shoulder and stops me mid-stride. First I look at his chest, because it's right in front of me, but then I look up at his face. His brows are drawn together, a deep line creasing down in between them. "Is something wrong?"

"You dated Blair?" I blurt it out like an accusation.

"You're upset about . . . *Blair*?" He says it like it's crazy. "That was last year."

"So what?" I take in a big breath. "What happened?"

"She was going through a lot. Her dad lost his job. They had a lot of money problems."

"And you dumped her?" I ask.

"No, she broke up with me."

Now I'm really confused. "Because you weren't there for her?"

"I tried to be, but when I quit football to help my dad out, suddenly I wasn't boyfriend material anymore. Everything was falling apart for Blair at home and I guess she couldn't stand the thought of her life at school going down the tubes, too. Dating the popular football star was part of who she needed to be."

"You were popular?" All this new information completely overwhelms me.

He laughs at the shock in my voice. "Playing football seemed to make up for my strange home situation. But when football was gone, so was Blair."

"Why does she hate you so much if she broke up with *you*?" I pull back a little so I can get a better look at his face.

"I'm not sure she hates me. I think she's just angry about things she couldn't control. I'm one of them."

"And you don't care?" Because I can't imagine not caring about Blair's opinion of me.

"Sure I do. But Blair's been getting mad at me since grade school about something or other. She'll get over it." He pushes a hand through his hair, then adds, "At least, I hope she will."

He glances back over my shoulder toward the flower shop. "Look. My grandmother and Mrs. Annie Florence want you to come over to the house on Saturday. I told them you're interested in *el Día de los Muertos*. They got all excited. You know how they are about that stuff."

I don't say anything right away and his phone buzzes, interrupting the tension between us.

"Sorry." He takes it out of his pocket. Whatever the message is makes him frown, but he looks back up at me quickly. "You'll come?"

I nod, reluctantly.

"Okay." He looks relieved, and then stuffs the phone back into his pocket. "I delivered the flowers, but I need to go. Sorry. Don't mean to rush you, but there's a call and I have to help my dad."

"What call?"

"That's what we say when somebody dies. We have to go out to the house and help remove the body."

"Oh," I say. Strangely enough, I'm not even weirded out by this. It just seems part of a strange new normal where Luis is concerned.

"Great. We'll talk on Saturday. Maybe we can catch a movie or something?" Luis offers casually, turning toward the van.

"I'd like that," I say, and realize I'd like it much more than I want to admit.

"I love being able to communicate every day to my followers." **—Torrey Grey, Beautystarz15**

CHAPTER EIGHTEEN

SURPRISING MAKEUP TRICKS

My eyes fly open and I am face-to-face with Stu. He is sitting on top of my rib cage staring at me. It takes me a minute to realize there are no skeletons, no moonstone-size holes in my chest, no bad dreams. Just one very heavy cat.

It's Saturday morning. I'm in my room and in my bed. I try to calm my ragged breathing.

"Meow," Stu says.

"Go away," I hiss, and squeeze my lids shut. I'm going to kill Raylene for leaving this cat here. I open my right eye. Stu is now nose-to-nose with me. He has a scary "I'll wait you out" kind of look on his face. He definitely isn't going anywhere.

"MEOW," he says as soon as I open one eye.

"I'm ignoring you," I say firmly.

He looks at me. Blinks. And then very slowly stretches out his two front paws and begins kneading the top of my blanket with his claws.

"Stop it!"

I push him away with both hands. It is like moving a big, fat, furry brick. He makes a circle down one of my blanket-covered legs and up the other, ending up settled back on my chest with a "Hrruuummpp."

We repeat this process several times, until I finally give up. He ends up comfortably curled on my chest, purring loudly in victory.

There is a knock at the half-opened door and both of us turn our heads to see who it is. Raylene pushes the door open wider and steps in. She's wearing a black tank top, leopard-skin leggings, and pink glitter flats.

"Your mom let me in. I left his carrier and some food in the kitchen," she says, looking down at me and Stu in the bed. She pulls a long string of bright purple chewing gum out of her mouth and sucks it back in slowly with an obnoxious slurping sound. I slide over to the other side of the bed. Stu balances on my stomach.

"I really think he likes you." Raylene sits down on the side of the bed we just left.

"Or really wants to punish me," I say. I stretch my arms up over my head and Stu rides out my movements like a good surfer on a wave.

"Your mom said to tell you she went to pick your dad up at the airport in Houston," Raylene says.

I'm surprised. Mom drove to the grocery store twice last week and once to Target. Little excursions. Baby steps. But driving to the airport is major progress. Houston is only a little over an hour away, but for my mom it must be like driving to New York City.

"She said they might stop off in Conroe on the way back and have lunch."

"Okay." But it's better than okay. Now I don't have to explain myself to anyone. I have the whole house to myself.

"She said to be sure and watch the cat." Raylene shakes her finger at Stu and he glares back at her. "Do not leave him alone to tear up anything in the house."

"I know, I know," I sigh.

"At the very least, I hope I make alternate," Raylene says, changing the subject in her way.

I suddenly remember the whole point of this cat-babysitting thing — the twirling thingy.

"Oh yeah. Me, too," I say, and then, because I can't stop myself, "Is that what you're going to wear?"

"What's wrong with it?"

"Nothing." What do I know about what twirlers are supposed to look like? This might be just the right outfit. I kind of doubt it though. And that teased-up bump of a hairdo has got to go. "Maybe you could do something different with your hair?" I suggest.

"Like what?"

"Maybe a fishtail braid on the side?" And then I say something that surprises even me. "I could do it if you want."

Raylene looks shocked, but then a slow grin spreads across her face. She nods slowly. "Okay."

Stu lets out a yowl of frustration as I push him off to the side and swing my legs off of the bed. My own reflection in the dresser mirror is depressing. I pick up a brush and try to pull it through the tangled mess of my morning hair, then give up. I'll deal with it later.

"Sit on the floor in front of me," I tell Raylene, and wait while she gets settled cross-legged on the carpet. It takes fifteen minutes to brush out her ratted-up bump and complete an intricate braid down one side of her shoulder. All the while, Raylene eats Snickers that somehow magically appear from some pocket, and screeches periodically that I'm pulling her hair. Stu watches it all from the top of my dresser like he couldn't possibly be more disgusted.

"It's beautiful," Raylene says finally as we both survey my hard work in the mirror. I have to agree. She reaches for me, but I manage to deflect the hug with one stiff arm.

"Don't mess it up," I say, but I smile back at her. Her hair looks so much better, if I do say so myself. It's been a while since I did this makeover thing just for fun. It reminds me why I started the whole beauty vlog in the first place.

"Oh, right." She nods. Then she turns to Stu and scratches him under his chin. "Be good," she tells him.

"Good luck!" I tell her as she's heading out the door. Rooting for Raylene was never part of the plan, but to my amazement, I mean it.

After she's gone, I pad down the hall through the now empty house toward the kitchen. Stu weaves wildly in and out of my legs, almost causing me to trip twice. I feed him some Mr. Purrfect and start to fix myself a peanut-butter-and-banana sandwich. But reaching for the bread, I see spaghetti noodles instead. I used to fix spaghetti for Miranda. It was the first thing I learned to cook — just the noodles and the sauce out of a jar — and it was her favorite. She was such a picky eater, but she would eat my spaghetti for breakfast, lunch, or dinner.

I eat spaghetti for lunch. With every bite, I remember Miranda. She feels so much closer to me now than we were in real life. She surrounds me.

I wander around the house a couple more times, but I can't shake the restlessness. I finally sit down on the dead-leaf-colored couch and try to let the television fill up my mind with other people's thoughts. It doesn't work. I flip the channel. It is a sports channel and two teams are playing softball. Miranda. I flip the channel. A nature show with chimps. Miranda. I flip the channel again. It is a cartoon with superheroes. Miranda. I turn off the television and let out a shaky breath. It is the same as in my head — all channels are set to Miranda.

Finally, I realize that Luis's invitation is a reason to get out of the house. I brush the tangles from my hair and cover up the dark circles under my eyes as best I can. Then I pull on skinny jeans, a lace tank, and layer on a baby-doll shirt. My black high-top Converse sneakers are under the bed, but I pull them out.

Stu strolls into the bedroom. If I leave him alone in this house, he will have a great big Stu party with Mom's cashmere throw in the living room and it will open up a whole big line of questions about where I'd been when Stu was destroying the house. I'm still not ready to talk to my parents, or anyone else, about Luis.

I look at Stu. He looks at me. He has to come along.

After some Mr. Purrfect bribery and one long scratch on my forearm, I finally get Stu into his purple harness and inside the carrier. He makes a horrible growling, yowling noise that I've never heard any kind of animal make before. I find the keys and manage to get the cat and the carrier out to the car.

I turn on the ignition and look down through the holes on the top of the crate into the angry green cat eyes.

"Meow," Stu tells me, and I drive.

"I think he's traumatized," Luis says. "Or maybe carsick?"

He's sitting this close to me on the couch and all he is thinking about is the cat?

"He's fine." I glare at Stu, who is stretched comfortably in Luis's lap. The house is filled with the smell of baking bread and I try to blame the overall impression of mouthwatering deliciousness on that and not on Luis's presence.

He scratches Stu under his chin and the cat closes his eyes, purring loudly. I glare at Stu. He ignores me, his purr getting louder. I can't seem to take my eyes off Luis's hands, watching his fingers caress the fur. A sudden lump forms in my throat and I swallow uneasily. What is happening to me?

I'm jealous of a cat? It's just that I can almost imagine what it feels like. . . .

"What?" I jerk my eyes up to Luis's face.

"I didn't say anything." He smiles at me, and I hope that he has no clue what I was just thinking.

"We're making *pan de muerto,*" Mrs. Annie Florence announces from the doorway. She's wearing an apron that says *Never Trust a Skinny Cook,* and waving a spatula. Her sudden interruption startles Stu from Luis's lap. He jumps to the floor with a thud and quickly finds a corner to soothe his ruffled fur.

"Have you ever had it?" Mrs. Annie Florence asks me.

I shake my head. "What is it?"

"It's like a sweet roll with sprinkled sugar on top and it's decorated with bones made of dough," Maria says, appearing beside Mrs. Annie Florence.

Who decorates bread with skeleton bones? People eat this stuff?

"Delicioso." Mrs. Annie Florence claps her hands together, her blue glasses wobbling wildly on the end of her nose. "It's just coming out of the oven. I like to serve it with guava jelly and burnt-orange marmalade."

"You definitely have to try it," Luis says, pulling me up off the sofa.

I follow them all out to a large sun-drenched kitchen. The smell of the baking bread permeates everything, and some kind of classical piano music is coming from a boom box plugged in under the open window over the sink. I take a seat on one of the barstools at a massive island. A huge vase of yellow marigolds sits on the countertop in front of me. The last time I saw marigolds was that day at the mall. I blink and look away.

Mrs. Annie Florence must have noticed my reaction. "Do you like the *cempasúchil* flowers?"

"They're beautiful," I lie.

"The ancient Aztecs used the *cempasúchil* flowers to honor the dead," Mrs. Annie Florence says. "Their colors represent the colors of the earth. On *el Día de los Muertos*, their scent is thought to guide the spirits back to the earth and to their homes."

I feel my heart squeeze.

Maria is at the stove. "I put those photos out for you to see," she tells me. "It's sugar-skull makeup. Luis told me about your makeup hobby, so I thought you might like them."

Makeup hobby?

I wonder exactly how that conversation went down, but don't ask because my eyes are drawn to the stack of photos on the counter. I'm completely captivated. Each one is a different close-up of a girl. Their faces are painted white, mouths "stitched" closed, and then decorated with elaborate flowers and hearts. I start thinking of what product to use to get the effect.

Pencil or gel liner? What to use for the foundation?

"You like it, *sí*?" Maria asks.

"Sí," I say, my eyes lingering on the bright heart noses

and the stitched black mouths. It shouldn't be beautiful, but it is. Dark and light. Color and shadow. Death and beauty.

Maria slides her hands into mitts and pulls the oven door open. A puff of hot air ruffles her white hair and sends even more amazing smells into the room. She carefully pulls out two baking sheets full of rounds of bread and puts them on the top of the stove.

"You're going to leave us some, right?" Luis says, leaning over her shoulder and taking a deep inhale. He looks back toward me. "She's making all of this for her Tejano Historical Society meeting. Not for me."

"*Pobrecito.* You might get a couple. If you're lucky and your grandmother loves you." Maria grins and then swats him out of her way. "Over there. I have to brush these with the glaze while they're still warm."

Luis joins me on a barstool.

"We're also decorating sugar skulls," Mrs. Annie Florence says. She places a box on the island, opens up the top, and starts taking out tubes of icing, foil, ribbons, and tubs of glittery decorations.

Great. More skeletons.

"I already did this one. You get a blank skull and then you make it . . . beautiful." Mrs. Annie Florence pulls out a white sugar face covered with bits of glitter. It has bright pink lipstick where the lips should be and a red bow iced in on top. She displays it proudly and then tries to hand it over for me to admire.

The mouth is laughing silently and the empty eye sockets remind me of my dreams. I don't want to touch it, but I don't know how to avoid it without hurting her feelings. I gingerly take it out of her hands and pretend to look closer.

"Can you eat them?" I ask, handing the skull back to Mrs. Annie Florence.

"Would you eat a Chanel or a Givenchy?" Maria asks in horror.

I'm surprised at her fashion knowledge, considering the *Star Wars* T-shirt she's wearing under the flowered apron.

"But Chanel and Givenchy don't make clothes out of sugar," I point out, and Luis chuckles.

Mrs. Annie Florence reaches back in the box and takes out a tiny chocolate skull covered with bright, primary-colored dots of icing.

"This one is for a child," she says. "Miniature candy skulls are made for the baby *angelitos* and put on the grave sites."

Warmth floods my face. Of course I think of Miranda. My *angelito.*

Mrs. Annie Florence puts out more and more tiny decorated skulls. One after another, appearing out of the box. They are surrounding me. I suddenly feel dizzy and a little sick to my stomach.

I remember last night's dream and there is a rushing sound in my ears.

"Are you okay?" Luis asks.

"I'm fine." I can feel the dampness of the cold sweat on the nape of my neck.

Tiny baby gravestones. Everywhere. I'm at the cemetery. But there are hands. Clawing up out of the dirt. Reaching toward me. Everywhere I turn, more hands. Bony skeleton fingers grasping at my ankles and my legs. The white disembodied heads are coming toward me and I can't escape.

I stand up suddenly, bumping into Mrs. Annie Florence. The jolt knocks the skull out of her hands and it falls to the floor with a crash, shattering into pieces.

"I'm sorry." I drop to my knees and try to pick up the broken, scattered pieces. Part of the face is in my hands. Pieces of eyes. A mouth.

"Look at me, Torrey." The voice breaks through the fog, and I glance up to see Luis. "Leave it," he says quietly. "It's not important."

I blink. It's not a nightmare. I spread my fingers and let the pieces of sugar fall to the floor. Luis's hand is stretched out to me and I take it slowly, pulling myself up to my feet.

"No worries." Maria is there with a dustpan and a broom. "I'll sweep this up. Why don't you go out on the porch? I'll bring some of the *pan de muerto* out there as soon as I get the sugar on top."

I follow Luis out the side door, trembling.

"At least it wasn't the one with the plaid bow." I hear Mrs. Annie Florence say behind me. "That one is my favorite."

"Always look for the potential of what could be, not what is."

—Torrey Grey, Beautystarz15

CHAPTER NINETEEN
DELICIOUS GLOSSES FOR KISSABLE LIPS

On the porch, Luis and I sit down on the swing. We rock in silence for a few minutes, the music from the kitchen drifting out through the windows.

"What happened back there?" Luis asks.

A sigh escapes me. I close my eyes, listening to the faint squeak of the swing as it rocks back and forth, tears gathering beneath my eyelids.

Luis says, "Sorry. If you don't want to talk about it, that's okay."

I do want to talk about it. That's the problem. I just have no idea how to start. "Those skulls reminded me . . ." My voice trails off and I pick at my fingernails, looking down at my lap.

I glance up and meet his eyes. He nods, trying to encourage me to keep talking.

"It just hit me wrong," I say.

His voice is so soft, his eyes so dark. "Maybe it's not a bad thing to remember."

"Maybe," I say, but I'm not sure. Remembering hurts. "It was nice of your grandmother and Mrs. Annie Florence to ask me over. I hope I didn't upset them."

"They're just happy to see me having friends over."

"Like Blair?" I hate that she's the first person that comes to mind, and hate it even more that I ask out loud.

"Blair never came to my house. She didn't want to talk about my family and what we did. Every time I had to work it was a huge argument. Everything about the funeral home was a taboo subject. Finally, I had to choose."

He pushes the swing back into motion. "Ross was the one who was always over here."

"Ross?" My mouth falls open. "He doesn't even speak to you."

"Yeah, that's my fault," Luis says. "We used to be friends. More like brothers. In middle school, we started making plans. We were going all the way to the state championship. I was going to throw him the game-winning touchdown."

"What happened?"

"I quit the team."

"Couldn't you explain to him though?" I ask. "About having to work?" But I'm thinking that I know all about losing a best friend.

"We didn't talk about it." He gives me a rueful grin. "*I* didn't talk about it. And then everything happened with Blair and it just seemed easier to avoid them all. I didn't want him to have to choose sides."

"You were avoiding *them*?" I shake my head in wonder, then think of Zoe and Cody. How it was a relief, in a way, to escape both of them. Leave them back in Colorado.

"I'm not proud of it," Luis says. "It just seemed like more trouble to try and fix things. So I didn't. I let him down."

"You could still make it right. They'd understand if you talked to them." I pick at the wood on the arm of the swing with one nail.

He shrugs.

We sway back and forth on the swing. I can tell Luis doesn't want to talk about Blair and Ross anymore.

"That sugar-skull makeup *was* cool," I say.

"I thought you'd like that," he says.

"That's why I got into all the makeup and fashion vlogs in the first place," I explain. "It felt so creative."

"And now?"

And now . . . I'm a public humiliation with thousands of critics commenting on my every move. At the touch of a screen, I'm fake, phony, stupid, conceited, or even worse. My hair is too straight. My voice is too perky. My eyes are too wide. I'm too tall. Too skinny. Too pale. Too . . . something bad and ugly.

"It got complicated," I tell Luis.

"There are always going to be people who don't like you."

I blink. Is he reading my mind now?

"Listen," he goes on. "You can't beat yourself up over the haters. You have to let it go."

"Maybe."

He leans over and says quietly in my ear, "No 'maybe.'"

I nervously push the swing into motion again. His words leave a prickle of awareness lingering on my neck and I can hardly think of anything else.

"I have something for you," he adds, pulling something out from his pocket. He hands me a small brown paper bag, tied with a red ribbon. I look up at him in surprise, then untie the ribbon. I reach inside and pull out the soft knitted material.

A pair of red socks with pictures of yellow and green socks on them.

Socks with socks.

My eyes instantly fill up with tears again. "Where did you find them?"

"An Internet search turned up a sock specialty store in Conroe. I didn't want to take the chance they wouldn't be right, so I drove down and picked them up. It was only an hour away," Luis says proudly.

I don't know what to say. I am suddenly aware of my own heartbeat, pounding wildly against the base of my neck. I close my eyes again. When I open them, Luis is sitting so close I can see his chest move up and down with each breath and I can't stand it any longer. Wrapping my arms around his neck, I kiss him.

I don't mean to. It certainly isn't planned. But at the same time, how can I not kiss him?

I can sense that he's surprised, too, but he kisses me back. He smells like soap and cinnamon. When Luis pulls slowly away, I can still feel the touch of his lips on mine.

He reaches out to slide his hands up either side of my face, pulling me close enough to feel him smile against my mouth. Sitting there with foreheads touching, I can't remember when I felt this happy. Certainly not with Cody. Maybe never.

"Thanks," I say, one hand lingering behind on his broad chest. And I mean thanks for listening and thanks for the socks and thanks for how his eyes darken right before he kisses me, and thanks for the way my heart pounds when I look at him. But I don't explain.

"Luis!"

We both look up. A tall man in a white lab coat is coming across the grass. I can immediately see the resemblance. His face is chiseled into the same sharp planes as Luis's.

"I just went to open a Pacific Pine casket and an entire cap ripped off the hinges. And the service is in four hours. I've got two people to dress and casket."

"This is my dad," Luis says to me. "Dad, this is Torrey."

The man nods, but obviously has more important things on his mind.

"Call the casket delivery guy and get me an emergency casket." He rushes off, giving me a quick "good-bye" and "nice to meet you" over his shoulder.

"Looks like I have to go to work," Luis says, standing up from the swing. I stand up beside him and he rests his hand on my elbow. "Sorry."

And I'm sorry, too, but not because he has to work. I'm sorry because he stops touching me.

"Hey, where did this cat come from?" Maria yells from the kitchen, and then says some words in Spanish I don't know, but also don't need Mrs. Annie Florence to translate.

Luis steps away from me with a big sigh. "I'll talk to you tomorrow?" he asks.

I nod. I give him a small wave and slowly step backward off the porch, stumbling slightly on the steps. I'm in a daze from our kiss.

The front door bangs open. "These are for you." Mrs. Annie Florence says, handing me a wrapped bouquet of marigolds.

Maria is behind her with an armful of yowling Stu. "And don't forget this cat."

"Sharing products you love is how fans get insight into your personality." **—Torrey Grey, Beautystarz15**

CHAPTER TWENTY

WHAT'S IN MY PURSE?

At lunch on Monday, I'm still thinking about Luis's kiss. Only now I'm also thinking, or more like worrying, about a lot of other things. Like how Blair is going to react if she gets any idea that I kissed Luis. The worst part is that, even though I know it will ruin all my plans for staying here at the popular table, all I can *really* think about is doing it again.

In English, Luis smiled at me from his regular seat across the room, but we didn't speak. While the teacher read aloud from some poem, I watched the back of Luis's head bent over a book, his hands twirling a pencil between his fingers. Then I caught myself and made myself look away so no one would notice. It happened at least three more times before the bell rang, and I escaped into the crowded hall before he could talk to me.

Ross and Max, the guy with the buzz cut, are arguing about some zombie movie that is showing at the midnight theater this weekend. Emily and Blair are oohing and aahing over pics of Mia's new Frye boots that she can't even wear until this weather turns cooler.

"It's going to happen this weekend," Blair says.

"I heard the temperature is dropping into the forties," Emily confirms.

Neither the thought of zombies or cooler weather interests me. I sit there in a fog, glancing around every five seconds to see if Luis is walking through the door.

"What's wrong with you today anyway?" Blair says, and I jerk my attention back to the table. Her brown eyes narrow.

"Nothing," I say, too quickly.

Emily chimes in, "You were completely out of it in English."

"I have a lot on my mind."

"I bet," Blair says.

I feel suddenly cold. *She knows about Luis.*

"If everyone was saying such terrible things about me, I'd be a complete disaster. Honestly, I don't know how you hold it together." Blair digs around in her purse, pulls out a pink lip gloss, and slides it over her lips. "I can't believe she was actually your friend."

It takes a minute for her words to sink in. She thinks my mood is about the video Zoe posted. So much has happened since then.

"Some friend," Emily repeats, nodding like a bobble-head doll.

"Your friend Zoe was in a lot of your vlogs, right?" Mia asks. "Like the one where you both showed what you had in your purses?"

"Yeah," I say, remembering that Zoe texted me again this morning. I ignored it, again.

"You filmed what you had in your purse?" Max is aghast. "And people watched it?"

"Thousands," I mumble.

"Oh, wow." Blair's expression is awestruck. "It would be so cool to be in one of your videos."

I stare back at Blair, feeling my adrenaline spike. In that instant, a plan starts to gel in my mind.

"Hey," Ross says to Max, "want to see what's in my pockets?"

"Wait." Max holds his hands out to stop Ross from reaching into his jeans pockets, and then looks wildly around the room. "Maybe everybody wants to watch this."

I don't pay attention to the boys. "You can be in my video," I tell Blair, and start to put the plan into action. It takes a little bit of a sales pitch to get Blair and Mia excited about the sugar-skull makeup tutorial, but soon they are convinced it's the coolest thing ever. Especially when I pull out my phone and show them the pictures I'd found online with flowers trailing around each eye and upside-down hearts for noses.

Emily says her mother wouldn't approve. So she's out. That's okay with me.

"Once the raw footage is edited, it'll be amazing," I say to Blair and Mia.

"And if you post this vlog right after the court appearance, it'll totally blow up. There's no telling how many page views we're talking about," Mia says. I feel uncomfortable because I know she's right and it sounds so callous.

"That would be so symbolic," Blair breathes, her eyes wide. "All the buzz about your statement and then . . . BOOM . . . this is the first thing you post. So beautiful and so sad."

I feel a twinge of guilt. My statement. I still don't have a script for that, but somehow all those pieces of memory stuffed away in my closet will come together in my mind. They have to. It'll be the most important haul I've ever presented. Only it won't be online. It will be in a courtroom in Colorado.

"And you'll tag us both?" Blair asks, biting her lower lip in anticipation.

I nod. That's the best part of this plan. It's going to make my real-time popularity soar, too. A total win-win.

"You'll be stars," I assure them. Then I hesitate. Maybe I can tie this all up into one big bow and please everyone. "On one condition."

"What?" Mia's eyes narrow suspiciously.

"You have to wear the makeup to Raylene's Halloween party. It's just across the street and I promised her you'd drop by." I haven't seen Raylene since she got back from the twirling contest (she placed second) and collected Stu. I've been able to drive myself to school now. But still. Raylene is my cousin. And it's more than that. Somehow Raylene matters to me now. Even if she's unpopular.

"Why?" Blair asks incredulously. She and Mia look at each other like it's the craziest thing they've ever heard.

I think fast. "I need to get some real reactions. Maybe film some background footage of you at a party. I can splice it in later."

"I think it sounds like fun," Ross says, and I look over with raised eyebrows. As far as I can tell, he isn't kidding.

"Well, we're not staying long," Mia huffs.

But they're coming. I don't know why, but this makes me smile.

For the rest of the week, as much as I want to talk to Luis in school — to kiss him again — I find myself avoiding him. Instead, I spend all my free time discussing the makeup-tutorial vlog with Blair and Mia. After school on Friday, I help Raylene get ready for the party.

In her usual Raylene fashion, she's going completely over the top. She invites people through Facebook, Twitter, texts, and even personal hand delivery. She wants to be sure she gets everything just right. Music. Food. Decorations. We almost break our necks stretching fake spiderwebs all across her porch and carving out a jack-o'-lantern to put on the top step.

I'm just praying people actually show up. I'm still counting on at least Blair and Mia.

My parents seem happy that I'm going to Raylene's party. Especially when I say some of my friends are coming over beforehand.

"Sounds like things are getting back to normal," my dad tells me with a half smile.

Right. Normal. Picking out a dress for a party. A room full of girls putting on makeup. The carpet littered with a wide array of shoe options. All normal. Just like when Zoe used to come over to get ready to go out.

Dad doesn't know about the backpack in my closet full of *ofrendas*.

Because that isn't normal at all.

The night of the party, I'm all nervous energy. I dig around until I find the green dress at the very back of the closet. Zoe picked this dress from a sales rack at Macy's. She said it would look fantastic on me and she was right. I loved the soft green color, the sweetheart neckline, the flared skirt. I only wore it once — for the Christmas card photo I took with Miranda.

I pull the dress on over my head. It still clings to me perfectly. Slipping on some black high heels, I stand in front of the mirror. I pin my hair up into a loose, messy bun and put some silver hoops in my ears. It's been a long time since I looked like this, but I remember this girl. She used to talk fearlessly into a camera and was addicted to checking her page views.

My dad pushes the door open and stands in the doorway. "Hey," he says.

"Hey."

"You look beautiful, honey."

"Thanks. It's the dress," I say.

"It's good to see you going out." He didn't say *for a change,* but I know it's hanging in the air.

"You're going to spend the night over at Raylene's?"

"She asked me. It's okay, right? I know it's the first time I've been away since . . ." My voice trails off. "But it's just across the street."

Raylene thought a sleepover would be a perfect end to her successful party. As far as I know, I'm the only one who is actually sleeping over. I hope the evening's going to be a success, but I have my doubts. The overnight might turn into a pretty desolate consolation party, and I'm going to be the one picking up the very random Raylene pieces.

"It's fine," Dad says. "We just have to take it slowly." His voice cracks a bit. I glance at him out of the corner of my eye. He pauses, as if searching for the right words to say, or maybe until the quiver in his voice stabilizes. I feel tears prickling my eyes and I blink hard to keep them from coming. His sudden show of emotion is unnerving. I remember how he cried that night in the hospital, when he told the doctor to unplug the machines keeping Miranda's body breathing.

"I'm sorry. It's just so hard to see you growing up and know she never will." Dad walks over to me, puts his arm around my shoulders, and pulls me into his chest. I feel the thud of his heart against my ear.

I bite my lip to keep from crying — angry at myself for the familiar sadness bubbling up between us.

Can't I be happy for a few hours?

But I don't say anything. Instead I turn and walk over to my dresser, fiddling with the camera for the vlog. My first vlog in ages.

"I saw the video Zoe posted."

My whole body freezes. I don't even breathe.

"It wasn't your fault, Torrey."

I wish I could believe that.

He continues, talking softly. "We've all said things we wish we could take back. I would give anything to have never said the doctors could turn off those machines."

I turn back to Dad. He looks so sad. Suddenly, I see his own guilt from that horrible night when he pleaded for the doctor to give us some other option — some plan.

"There was nothing you could do," I say quickly. Miranda wasn't fixable. I reach out for his hand and his fingers wrap around mine, squeezing tightly.

"Thanks, hon," he says.

The doorbell rings and I hear Mom greeting Blair and Mia. Dad kisses the top of my head and leaves the room. I take a deep breath, then finish screwing the flip cam on a tripod stand and focus it on the two chairs I have ready. The flip cam gives me a little different angle than the webcam on my laptop, but still won't be the quality of Zoe's camera.

For now, I'll just film everything without pausing. I'll download the footage onto my computer later for editing.

"Torrey! Your friends are here!" Mom calls.

Are they my friends? I push the thought away. *Of course they are.*

I hear Blair and Mia tromping down the hall in their high heels. It's showtime.

"Post often. Viewers want to know you're going to be dependable." —**Torrey Grey, Beautystarz15**

CHAPTER TWENTY-ONE

HALLOWEEN SHOPPING FOR THE FASHION CONSCIOUS

Blair comes in first with a big, excited grin. She gives me a hug, which puts me more at ease. Meanwhile, Mia is scoping out my room.

She turns around slowly, her hands on her hips. "Big change from your bedroom back in Colorado," she says. "No pink. No pillows. No designer duvet."

I shrug. "I don't see the sense in spending a lot of effort decorating a rental. We'll be moving soon anyway," I say. But I have no idea if this is true or not. I point to the two wooden ladder chairs. "We'll film against that blank wall. I'll keep the shot tight and focus on your faces."

For the first time since she entered the room, Mia smiles. "So this is going to be your big comeback vlog?"

"Yeah," I say, straightening the pots and brushes spread out on the folding table I set up earlier. My hands tremble with anticipation. I shake out the nerves, clench and unclench my fingers.

Mia sneezes suddenly. Once. Twice. "Do you have a cat?"

"No, why?"

"I'm allergic" — she sneezes again — "to cats."

I could hug Stu right about now. Evidently he left some fur behind last weekend. "There's some Kleenex on my dresser."

"This is going to be epic," Blair says, taking the chair I indicate. Mia sits next to her. Thankfully, both are clean-faced and makeup free, as I asked them to be. They also remembered to wear something fairly simple to keep their faces as the main focal point. Mia is in a solid blue skater dress and silver pumps. Blair wears a dress I recognize as Kate Spade. The top is solid black with a full, black-and-white-striped skirt that hits just above her knees. It's a good choice to show off the skull makeup. I just hope they are as good at following direction with the rest of the shoot.

I see a glimpse of white at the back of Blair's collar.

"Oops. Your label is showing. Want me to cut it off for you?" I reach for it and then realize it's not a label, it's a price tag.

Blair shrugs away from my touch. "Just tuck it in," she says to Mia. "I have to return this tomorrow."

Mia sneezes again and does as she's told.

This is it. The tingle in my fingers spreads into my hands. I'm back in front of a camera. I turn away and take three long breaths, blowing them out one by one. It's different than when I tried to film before. Now I have an audience right in front of me. There are expectations and impressions to make. I push RECORD and start talking.

"Hey, Beauty Stars! Long time no chitchat, right? But today I have a special treat for you featuring my new friends Blair and Mia." I swivel the camera around. "Say hello, ladies."

"Hey." Blair waves at the camera and smiles.

Mia giggles a little and raises a hand in salute. "Hi," she sniffs.

I can't wait for Zoe to see this video. To see my new popular friends here in Texas. I remember Zoe's sobs on the phone and my stomach tightens. Then I try to push her from my thoughts.

"So tonight we're doing a haunting, yet joyful look for Day of the Dead." I narrate from the back side of the camera. "Think of it as sort of high-couture Goth."

"Perfect for those fall costume parties," Blair says, and Mia snorts beside her, then giggles nervously.

Great. This is going to take forever.

"Let's start with Blair," I say, picking up the jar and putting it directly in front of the camera lens so viewers can see the brand. Because I'm not working on my own face, I can easily describe each step of the process while I actually do it.

The white stage makeup goes on thick and I smooth it out in quick strokes, blending it into Blair's temples. Then I move on to Mia. I talk while I work, and soon both girls' faces are covered with the white foundation.

"Contour your cheekbones with some of the dark gray eye shadow," I continue, leaning over Blair. I'm in the zone. Everything is coming back to me and I feel myself relaxing.

"Draw around your eyes with black liner and then color in the circle. Do the same thing on the other side."

Blair's and Mia's faces start to transform into the stuff of my nightmares, with dark black eye sockets and gaunt cheeks. But this time I'm in control of what's happening. My fingers tingle. "I know this looks pretty gruesome right now, but just wait. All the real fun is just beginning."

I move back and forth from Mia to Blair, repeating each step a second time and keeping the process the same on each girl. I'll probably cut some of this, but I know more footage is better than not enough. Mia sneezes a few times — I'll have to edit those out — but Blair sits perfectly still, like she is afraid any movement might mess me up.

"Now start decorating your face. Draw bright-colored flowers around your eyes and maybe an upside-down heart as a teardrop from one eye." I fill in the petals on Mia's cheekbone with red sparkling liner and draw green, leafy vines across her forehead. "Add a deep wine color for your lips and draw in some black lines for the stitching on your mouth."

I pull away from my creations. They look better than I ever expected. "Voilà. A perfect look to wear to any costume party."

And that's it. My vlog. As it always was. As if nothing has happened in the intervening months.

But what about Miranda? Shouldn't you say something?

But I don't. Instead we do one final shot of the three of us, me in the middle flanked by Mia and Blair in complete sugar-skull makeup. We all look into the camera and shout, "Happy Halloween!"

I push the STOP button on the camera, and Mia and Blair almost knock me over to get to the full-length mirror on the back of my closet door.

"This is amazing," Blair keeps saying.

"I wonder how many views we'll get," Mia says.

"Let's watch it now," Blair says.

"It's going to take a lot of editing," I say, storing the camera and tripod away in the corner. "Besides, we don't have time right now. Raylene's expecting us across the street."

Mia's painted lips dip down into an exaggerated frown. "We're all dressed up and going to that lame party. We need to go somewhere cool and spooky."

"Like a cemetery," Blair says.

"Or a mortuary," Mia says.

"Ohhhhh. Yeah. That'd be so cool for your background shots," Blair tells me, her eyes shining. "Way better than some stupid party."

"Raylene's party isn't going to be stupid." I surprise myself by saying it out loud, but I'm not sorry.

"I've never been to a mortuary before," Mia says. "Did you go there with Luis, Blair?"

I'm tense, waiting for her answer.

Blair picks up my brush off the dresser and combs through her hair, still fascinated by her face in the mirror. "I avoided it like the plague. It wasn't easy since Luis was over there all the time," she says, then looks at me. "But you've been there, right?"

It's like a trick question.

"Once. Just to pick up some stuff for my sister's service." I don't know why I lie, but then I have to make it even worse. "I heard there was this secret way to get in after hours. You know, when no one else is there."

"That would be *so* cool," Mia says. "You absolutely have to show us, Torrey." Suddenly she's being sweet to me.

"I will. I will," I promise, with absolutely no intention of ever following through. "But right now, we have a party to go to."

With all the time it took to finish their faces, there's no time left for me to do anything to my own face but a quick smoky eye look and some pink lip gloss. I finally get Blair and Mia to stop staring in the mirror, but pulling them away is like pulling teeth. I know it's only the idea of showing off that finally gets them across the street.

Mom and Dad are at the door when we leave, giving out candy to a ballerina, a ghost, and some kind of dragon-looking thing.

"You should take a jacket," Mom tells me, after she and Dad ooh and aah over Blair's and Mia's makeup. "There's supposed to be a storm later when the northern blows through."

I'm surprised she is thinking ahead. It's a good sign. "I'm just across the street. I'll come back and get one later if I need it."

Halfway across the street, I glance back to see my parents standing in the open door. My dad puts his arm around my mom and she leans into him, holding a plastic pumpkin full of tiny bags of Skittles out for the next round of trick-or-treaters. They almost look happy.

Sounds of music and laughter pour out of Raylene's house. Mia and Blair stand on the porch with their arms around each other's shoulders, giggling in anticipation of the reaction on the other side of the door. I take a deep breath and ring the bell.

"I'll get it," someone inside yells, and the door is thrown open. Ross stands there wearing a baseball hat that reads *I'd Rather Be Bowhunting.* Evidently this is his costume. His thick log of an arm is thrown casually over Raylene's shoulders and the top of her cat ears only comes to his chest. Interesting couple. If they are, in fact, a couple.

"Welcome," Ross says in his heavy Texas drawl. He makes a grand gesture with one sweeping arm to usher us into the living room. "Nice face paint," he says to Blair and Mia.

"Thanks!" they giggle, preening.

Raylene squeals appreciatively over the makeup. I can tell Blair is pleased. She moves past me and the crowd parts in awe. It's quite the entrance. Everyone is watching us, and it feels good. Like it used to feel when I had tons of page views and "likes" on one post.

In the corner, I spot Luis laughing with Denise Patton, a Goth from our English class who is ironically dressed like a princess. He doesn't seem to see me yet. A fresh wave of confusion rolls through me. He looks so handsome. He's not in a costume, he's just wearing a crisp white cotton shirt stretched across his broad shoulders and tucked into his jeans. All I can think of is that kiss we shared, and I'm instantly nervous. I can't avoid him forever.

"Photo op!" Blair squeals, and she pulls Mia in for a hug while she snaps pictures of the two of them with her phone at arm's length. I feel a twinge of jealousy, even though they are my own creation.

Blair has to stop taking pictures, though, because Mia starts sneezing. Her eyes are watery and red. I warn her not to rub them, since that will smudge the makeup. Then I hide my smile, wondering where Stu is lurking.

I dodge a couple of plastic spiders hanging from the ceiling and scan the room. There must be more than thirty kids crowded into Raylene's small living room. It's a weird mix — probably because of Raylene's frantic invitation system. There are some band geeks in one corner and a small huddle of nervous-looking freshmen hanging out over by the food. Some kids went all out on the costumes. Others, not so much. I recognize a couple of vampires and a zombie nurse, but I have no idea about the identity of the Incredible Hulk.

Next to Ross, Raylene is the highest in social rank at this party, and that's not saying much. It doesn't look like Blair Cunningham's kind of party.

Blair must reach the same conclusion because she turns to me and announces, "We're only going to stay for a few minutes. Then we're going to some other party across town that actually starts at a normal time." She looks around the room while she's talking. This is the first I've heard of another party.

"Hey," I hear Ross say to Raylene. "*I* think it's a great party." He gives her a fist bump, then ambles over to the food table.

Raylene is beaming.

I turn to her, lowering my voice. "Are you . . . ?" I ask, nodding my head toward Ross.

Raylene shrugs.

"I guess stranger things have happened," I say.

She grins and hands me a cupcake with a black plastic spider on top. "Can you get some more ice from the kitchen? There's a pitcher on the top of the fridge."

"Sure," I say, and then she's halfway across the room and headed back toward Ross.

"God. I think they are actually together." Blair is suddenly by my side, watching Ross and Raylene. The sneer on her face just makes me mad.

These are the people I want as friends? What does that say about me?

"I think they make a cute couple," I say, and don't care that she huffs back at me in response. It feels good to disagree with Blair. For once. "I have to get some ice."

I put the uneaten cupcake on the table and head down the hall toward the kitchen, leaving Blair staring after me in shock. I hear Mia sneezing and sneezing behind me.

Stu sits in the middle of the hallway, completely unfazed by all the noise.

"Hey, buddy," I say to him. He just blinks up at me. "You're doing a great job with all that fur. For your prize, I promise to keep you supplied with Mr. Purrfect and take your blingy purple harness off every time I can." I lean down to scratch him under his chin and he raises his head, eyes closing to happy slits. "I even promise that, every once in a blue moon, you can come over on Saturday mornings and cuddle."

In the kitchen, I have to stand on my tiptoes to get the plastic pitcher off the top of the fridge. The bag of ice is completely frozen into one huge chunk, so I lug it over to the sink and open a drawer to look for something to break it up into smaller pieces.

"Good job on the skull makeup. I can tell you've been doing some *Día de los Muertos* research. Very impressive," Luis says, coming into the kitchen behind me. I turn to look at him and blood rushes into my cheeks.

"I didn't think you saw us come in," I say, feeling awkward.

"I saw you," Luis says, watching me steadily.

I say something. He says something back. I have no idea what.

"You seem nervous," Luis says, stepping closer to me. "And you've been avoiding me all week."

I don't deny it. I can't. I swallow the pulse back down into my throat. "I'm sorry."

"I'm sorry, too," he says, his dark eyes softening. "I didn't mean to upset you the other day."

"You're not upsetting me." I lean in toward him like he's a magnet. Then I say way more than I intend to. "I'm just confused."

Luis smiles. "You know what the cure for that is?"

I shake my head.

"Dancing." With one smooth move, he takes my hand and lifts my arm high above my head. Before I can say a word, he twirls me around right there in the middle of the kitchen.

"This may be hard for you to believe — as big as I am — but I'm an excellent dancer," he says, looking down at me with a mischievous smile. Suddenly, he spins me out across the kitchen and then rolls me back up tight against his chest. I wrap my arms around his neck and hold on to keep from landing in a heap on the floor. The kitchen isn't the best place for dancing, but I can't help but laugh.

"I believe you," I say, looking up into his smiling face. Suddenly I realize I'm not jittery anymore and that I really, really like Luis Rivera.

"If you guys want to dance, you should move into the living room. Lots more room out there." Ross stands in the kitchen doorway with a big grin on his face, Raylene by his side. I feel the heat rise into my face again, but Luis doesn't pull his arms away.

"We're coming. Just give us a second," Luis says, still looking at me, not at Ross. I should care that we've been seen together, but at this moment I don't.

"Come on," Raylene says, laughing and pulling Ross back toward the rest of the crowd. "Leave them alone."

We're by ourselves in the kitchen again, but I know someone else could come in at any moment. I hear Mia's high-pitched laughter from the other room and someone turns up the music even louder. I look up at Luis, and see he is watching my reaction closely. He runs his fingers lightly through my hair. Then he kisses me. And I melt into mush.

When he finally pulls away, I feel breathless. His eyes look darker than ever. He slides his hands down my arms until his fingers find mine, intertwining. I want to stay here like this, leaning into him, for the whole night or, better yet, walk into the living room holding his hand proudly for everyone to see. But I can't do that.

"Don't you want people to like you?" I ask, because I realize it's really important to me that people do. Especially Blair and her group.

Luis gives half a laugh, pulling away and looking down at me. "Why does it matter?"

Because I don't want to have to choose.

I know I'm being silly, but it does matter. If they were all friends once, they could be again. "Couldn't you just talk to them? *Try* to make things better?"

"Some people thought it wasn't the right decision to leave the team without a quarterback, but it was my decision to make." He shrugs. "Why do you care so much?"

He won't even *try* to fix things? How am I supposed to be

with him? I look away. When I look back, his eyes seem colder. Changed.

"You don't have to be so different from everyone else," I tell him, trying to make him understand. "It's like you don't even care what people think."

"I care what some people think." Luis takes a step back from me, dropping my hands. "Just not everyone."

He looks a little sad now, but I don't stop. "You act like you're so deep and important," I say, because I'm angry. Not because it's true.

"I *am* someone important." His voice is low. I squeeze by him, but he reaches out for my elbow and then leans in close to add softly, "And so are you. Even without the cameras and the makeup."

I shake his hand off my arm and walk out of the kitchen.

The party is even more crowded. I hurry over toward the food table and self-consciously pour a cup of punch. It is some kind of tropical Kool-Aid concoction that tastes horrible. I sit it down on the table after only one sip.

"So you and Luis, huh?" Raylene is suddenly beside me. She smushes her two index fingers together and makes kissy noises. "I knew it!"

"It's nothing," I say, still upset from what just happened in the kitchen. I wonder where Luis is now, but I don't want to look behind me.

"So . . ." As usual, she's not easy to get rid of. "Does Blair know about this?"

"There's nothing to know about."

She makes a huffy-puffy sound. "Honestly, Torrey, you don't have to be so mean."

I feel a twinge of guilt. I hear Miranda's voice in my head. *Queen of mean.* "I'm sorry," I tell Raylene. "Oh God, and I forgot the ice."

But before I can brave the kitchen and the possibility of seeing Luis again, Blair and Mia appear.

"Let's go," Blair says, rolling her eyes. "We're done with this party."

"Want to come with?" Mia asks. I can't believe I actually heard her right.

"Remember how you said you knew how to get into the funeral home?" Blair says.

I nod, worried for what is going to come next.

"You're going to let us in. That's where we need to film the background shots."

My hands suddenly feel clammy. I can't do that to Luis.

"What about that other party?" I ask Blair. "Aren't you going?"

"I just made that up to get out of here," she whispers with a wicked grin. "Let's go to the funeral home!"

"Whooooooo!" Mia makes an exaggerated ghost noise, her hands waving wildly in the air, and sneezes. She looks around suspiciously, but still misses Stu sitting calmly under the coffee table.

"Maybe we shouldn't . . ." I start to say, but I don't have a chance to continue because Luis is now walking up to me. My whole body freezes. I'm more afraid he's going to put his arm around my waist or something in front of Blair than I am about breaking into the funeral home.

But Luis doesn't touch me. He only nods at me and says, "Hey."

I don't answer.

"You coming, Torrey?" Blair asks, ignoring Luis.

I take a step away from him and cross my arms. He looks puzzled for a second, then gives a slight frown of understanding. That tiny change of expression cuts into my heart.

I have a choice to make. Leave with Blair or stay with Luis.

It's like a line drawn in the sand.

"I love making friends all over the world."

—Torrey Grey, Beautystarz15

CHAPTER TWENTY-TWO

DON'T GET STUCK IN A FASHION RUT

The Rivera Funeral Home is dark and only the hearse is parked outside in the circle drive. It must be a slow night for death. Maybe the spirits are all getting ready for *el Día de los Muertos* celebrations around the world.

I pick up the mat and slide the key out into the porch light. It turns easily in the lock and I open the door wide. The dimly lit staircase going up into the mortuary is empty. There's no sign of anyone, dead or alive. I guess the Rivera family is all next door — there are a few lights on in upstairs windows — or out celebrating. The thought of getting caught is scaring me almost as much as what's inside.

Blair and Mia are waiting around the corner as instructed. I cup my hands around my mouth and call out softly. "All clear."

I said I would check it out and make sure no one was around, but the truth is I still have some conscience and didn't want them knowing how to get in anytime they wanted.

"Wow," Blair says. Her eyes gleam, and in that second I don't regret bringing them here. I have Blair's approval. All is as it should be.

"Welcome," I say, then let out a spooky laugh like we're in some geeky horror film.

"How cool is this?" Mia whispers, gazing around. "Nobody's going to believe we came here."

I want to say that they really shouldn't tell anyone, but I hold my tongue.

At the top of the stairs is a reception area full of couches and comfortable chairs, dimly lit with recessed lighting. An old-fashioned chandelier hangs unlit from the ceiling and chocolate-colored velvet curtains are drawn across the big picture windows. There is a series of doors leading off the larger room. Mia pushes open one door to reveal a chapel-like room with rows of pews. For funeral services.

Don't think about Miranda. Don't think about Miranda.

Mia closes the door and it slides shut without a sound. Nothing makes noise here — not even our footsteps on the thick carpet. I don't know what's worse — the silence, or the idea there might be some kind of horrible creaking or thud. If I listen hard enough, the quiet actually has a sort of humming sound of its own. It's not familiar and I don't like it.

"Where do you think they keep the dead people?" Mia whispers, and Blair giggles.

This was a mistake. We shouldn't be here. But before I can say anything, Blair is moving away from me, pushing through a set of doors and leading the way down a side hallway. Mia follows her, their made-up skeleton faces eerily floating through the dimness. My heart is pounding and I keep looking behind me just in case someone is there.

"You guys," I call out, following after them. "We should go."

Blair is opening doors and turning lights on and off. It's going to attract attention from anyone passing by in a car. Then she stops suddenly and I practically run into her back.

"Oh. My. God. Look at this." She holds a large metal door open and we all stand in the doorway. Inside it looks sort of like an operating room. Lots of gleaming silver and trays of instruments. Three large metal tables are in the middle of the room. Big showerheads hang from the ceiling over each one.

"It's to wash off the blood," Blair says.

Mia squeals and Blair hisses for her to be quiet. "Go inside," Blair says.

"Not me. You go inside."

"I'll do it," I say, and I do. I walk to the middle of the room and stand between the two metal tables. I turn around slowly with my arms outstretched. My heart is pounding. Trying my best to sound calm, I say, "No big deal. See? Now can we go?"

Blair puts her hands on her hips and smiles just the tiniest bit.

I realize then that I no longer care. "I want to go back to the party," I tell Blair. It feels good to say something so unpopular. "You guys go wherever you want."

Then the lights go out.

"Sorry this lighting is so bad," Mia says in the dark, and she laughs.

I hear the click of the door.

"Wait," Blair says, her voice muffled by the door.

"Come on." I can hear Mia's voice outside. "Leave her."

"We can't do that," Blair says, but then she laughs. "Okay. Go. Go."

I run forward. It's so dark, I can't even see my hands grasping at the hard closed door in front of me. I make myself blink a few times, seeking some shades in the darkness, but the total pitch black remains.

In the far-off distance, I hear laughter and the sound of a car honking, then silence.

They left me.

The realization slams into my brain.

Don't panic. Don't panic.

I close my eyes and try to calm my breathing, but the darkness is like dirt pouring in from the ceiling over my body and into my hair. It covers my face, filling up my nose. I open my mouth, but instead of air I suck in clumps of sand and dirt. I can't breathe. My eyes fly open, but there is no difference. The grinning skeletons surround me, their bony fingers stretch out to touch me at any moment. I feel them getting closer in the blackness.

There is nothing to do but give in. I sink down onto the cold concrete floor and start to cry, my sobs coming out in ragged raw sounds that don't even sound human.

Luis probably hates me. I hate me. There's nothing I could say that will make it right between us. There is no excuse for how I've treated him, or Raylene, or anyone else for that matter. I'm a shallow, bad person who deserves to be shut up in the dark. No wonder Zoe betrayed me. Mia and Blair are just like her. And, once again, I was so stupid I couldn't see what was coming.

I don't know how long I sit there crying, but finally the sobs stop, and then, gradually, the tears stop, too. No skeletons. No ghosts. Nothing but darkness. I brush away the wetness from my face with my hands, taking deep, steadying breaths. The contours of my cheekbones under my fingertips suddenly remind me of the sugar skulls, but here in the dark there are no flowers or glitter. There is only what lies below the surface of my skin. Unseen and unviewed. Hidden out of frame and focus.

In the absence of all noise comes the memory of sounds. Just the other day at the 7-Eleven I heard this little girl laugh. It sounded so much like Miranda, I had to put my cherry Slurpee down and walk to the back of the store just to make sure it wasn't her. It wasn't. But I realized I still remembered what Miranda's laugh sounded like — I hadn't forgotten. I try to remember more. In the dark, a lifetime of sounds suddenly crawls into my mind on endless playback. It is the language of sisters.

I get the front seat.

She started it.

Leave me alone.

Can you help me?

I'm going to tell.

She touched me!

Be that way.

I'm scared.

The voices twist and weave through the dark, then disappear. Once again I am alone and the silence presses in hard against my ears. I stand up, swaying a little, and stagger over, arms outstretched and waving wildly in front of me, to find the closed door. The cold surface is finally in front of me against my spread fingers, unyielding. I beat against it frantically, first with open slaps and then with clenched fists.

"Let me out!" I scream. I wait with my ear pressed against the door to listen for a response. There is nothing. I do it again. Still nothing.

Sliding my hands down the hard surface, I find the doorknob. One twist and it turns easily in my shaking hands.

I was never trapped inside. It was within my power to get out all along.

All I had to do was open the door.

I walk out of the funeral home and down the driveway in a daze. Blair and Mia are nowhere in sight, and I'm glad about that. There's a flash of light in the distance and it takes a minute to realize it's lightning. There's another and then another. The lightning is still too far away to hear the thunder, but coming closer. It doesn't matter. A storm could be raging all around me and I wouldn't even care. I'm not feeling much of anything. I'm just walking the blocks back to my house.

It takes a while, but the closer I get, the more sure I am of what I need to do next.

Music is still coming from Raylene's house, but it looks like the party crowd is dwindling. Through the open windows, I see her slow dancing with Ross, a huge smile on her face. Good for her. I'm glad someone is happy tonight. I don't see Luis, but I don't look long.

I slip into my dark house and down the hall to my bedroom, trying not to make any noise. My parents' door is closed and hopefully they are already asleep. I'm careful, closing my bedroom door softly and then turning on the light. I quickly change out of my rumpled party dress and into jeans and a T-shirt. I pull a hoodie out of the drawer just in case the weather turns, like everyone's been talking about. Grabbing the yellow marigolds out of a vase on my dresser, I wrap them up carefully in some tissues.

The clock says 11:00 p.m. One hour until midnight and the *angelitos* are released from heaven. I have just enough time.

"I just want to be real." —**Torrey Grey, Beautystarz15**

CHAPTER TWENTY-THREE
THE VERY BEST WATERPROOF MAKEUP

Every noise seems exaggerated in the still night. The sound of the car door slamming. The thump of the trunk after I pull out the backpack full of Miranda's things. The crunch of my shoes on the gravel road. The squeak of the half-open iron gate leading into the cemetery. In front of me the faint white rows of stones are visible behind the fence. There is supposed to be a full moon tonight. When it comes up it should give me plenty of light. As long as the thunderstorm stays to the north. I glance up. The pine trees stretch up into darkness and then branch out in Christmas tree tops, leaving only small visible patches of starry night.

I make my feet move forward in the darkness. I'm suddenly conscious of so many bodies lying there under my footsteps. My heart beats faster. Once they each had a heart that beat, too, and a chest that rose and fell with breath. Now they outnumber me in their complete stillness. Tonight, I'm the only one breathing.

I glance around again, nervously. There is no sign of a

moon yet, but there is a rumbling — low and long — in the distance. Thunder. The storm is closer and I'm grateful for the flashlight I tucked inside the sleeping bag. I look up at the still clear sky and almost immediately hear the thunder again. Louder. A little closer.

The lightning bolt comes out of the sky like a rocket and hits a pine tree at the back of the cemetery with a crash that shakes the ground. I can feel the electricity in the tips of my hair. I smell the burned wood just before the top of the tree tumbles into the underbrush, leaving behind a smoldering stump. Every particle of air is supercharged and vibrating and the reality of the situation hits me. I'm alone in a graveyard with a thunderstorm looming.

My hands shake something awful as I stretch out the tarp and tie it to the trees the way I learned on a Girl Scouts camping trip when I was ten. I unroll my sleeping bag and then sit back against the roughness of the tree trunk, the tarp my only protection overhead. *Ready*. There is a rustle of branches in the dark and I glance up. It's just the wind, but it whips wildly at the tarp. I hope my knots hold.

Every few minutes, the lightning illuminates everything, the surrounding gravestones stark white against the deeper dark. Then the cemetery crashes back into darkness, leaving behind only the clatter of thunder echoes. Each time, I count under my breath the space between to try to judge how close the thunder is. Each time it grows shorter. Above me, the tree trunks now reach up into a black, angry-looking sky.

I pull the hood of my hoodie up over my head, and the sides of my sleeping bag up around my legs. There is a rushing sound in the leaves overhead. The rain is definitely coming. I hear it smacking into the treetops first. In only a few minutes the drenching downpour reaches the top of the tarp, then pours over the side in hundreds of tiny rivers. But the tarp holds and I stay dry underneath it.

The deluge lasts only a short time, and then the rain hushes into a rustling shower on the canvas above me. The thunder quiets into dull rumbles, the lightning moves off into distant flashes. I sit and watch the last of the shower dripping off the leaves and trickling down stone monuments. Even in my current surroundings, the sound of the water is calming, and I remember.

We took Miranda to the ocean for the first time when she was four. Sand castles and seaweed. Hot dogs and hermit crabs. Those tiny angel wings that sparkle like purple jewels in the sand, and the glorious sound of the sea. It was all new to her.

For me, at age eight, it was delightfully familiar. First out of the car, I ran to the water's edge and stood, arms outstretched like the wind-stilled birds above me. I couldn't hear anything but the wonderful roar of the sea. I didn't want to hear anything else. Sometimes I could almost hear a mother calling to her child, or a man to his dog, or the seagulls, but it didn't matter. The sound of the ocean covered it all.

Mesmerized by the splash of the sparkling water, Miranda ran in and out of the crashing waves on her chubby little legs, squealing for me to join her. I wasn't going to stay in the shallows though. I wanted to be out in the action. The trick was to figure out exactly where the wave would break, but if I hit it just right I could ride the top almost to shore. It was an incredible feeling — the water churning and roaring beneath me as it carried me in to the shore. Then it passed over me and I was left sputtering for air while the wave crashed on toward Miranda, waving her hands wildly for me to come in and build a sandcastle.

I should have listened to her, but there were a lot of things I should have done. I should have played with her. I should have laughed with her more.

The trip to the beach was forgotten until now, but tonight is not about forgetting. I'm not fighting it anymore. I want to remember. *El Día de los Muertos.* The Day of the Dead. The time to remember.

My hands clench, pressed tight against my forehead, and I am suddenly intensely aware of the breath going in and out of my body. But I know there is a moment when the breath stops. I saw it that night at the hospital, squeezed between my grief-stricken parents, as we waited for the inevitable. One minute the chest rises. Air goes in. Then air goes out. But then it doesn't happen again. One moment there is life. The next there is only a shell.

When is that moment that the breath stops? How is that decided? What happens?

I can't stand it anymore. The questions pour out into the dark and the tears come down my face. One after another, I ask them aloud, my voice cracking with emotion.

"Where are you, Miranda? Is it dark? Are you afraid?"

Picking up the backpack from the ground in front of me, I step out from under the tarp. The rain has stopped, but the air is cooler. The moon is now visible at times through the trees. I don't know if it's full, but it's definitely big enough to light up the graveyard with a bluish light. The flashlight is dim in comparison. I turn it off and place it back under the tarp on the sleeping bag.

I wonder if there is a right way to do this. According to what I learned from Luis, I'm supposed to decorate and clean the grave. I bend over and brush away some leaves and sticks off the top of Miranda's tombstone. I can't help looking over my shoulder every few minutes. The moonlight casts rows of tombstone shadows on the dark, wet ground. Every piece of stone stands, no matter how old, a mute tribute to left-behind survivors just like me.

Whatever made the dead happy in life, they are to have again.

I take a deep breath and sink down to my knees, immediately feeling the damp seep into my jeans. Slowly, I open the backpack and reach inside. First I pull out the marigolds, hoping their scent is indeed an ancient path for Miranda's spirit to follow back to the living world. The bright gold color is a stark contrast to the dirt on the top of the grave.

I reach inside again and take out the first item — a blue baby blanket with a big yellow duck on the front. My hands don't shake as I carefully place it on the dirt in front of me, talking out loud in the dark. "You were always full of life and curiosity. You could have been a scientist and discovered the cure for cancer."

I take out the drawing of Sensational Sister next and unfold it carefully, laying it beside the blanket. "You were creative and artistic. Your favorite color was blue. You could have grown up to paint masterpieces that people would have lined up to see. Or invented a whole new superhero for girls everywhere."

Am I doing it right?

The softball shirt is next. "You were brave and would face any challenge put before you with determination and courage. You could have been the firefighter who rushed into a building to save the lives of many. Or a great athlete, playing a sport she loved."

At first it's weird talking out loud, but I start to get used to it.

Finally, I place the socks with socks out on the dirt. "You were funny and your laughter will forever be missed. You could have written stories and songs to entertain the future."

I'm soaked now and starting to shiver, but I have one more thing to do.

At first my voice is soft. "When the moon shines bright."

I pause for a moment to swallow, clearing my throat, and then continue. "Your fears will be few."

I close my eyes and then slide my hand deep into my jeans pocket for the last remaining item.

One moonstone bracelet.

I carefully place it at the bottom of the tombstone, right underneath the date when my world went crazy.

"And only sweet dreams will come to you," I whisper aloud.

I wrap the dry sleeping bag around my legs and sit back down under the tarp. The full moon rises into the clearing of trees above me, and I wait for the time when the living and the dead are supposed to reunite.

But no ghosts emerge. There is only the sound of my ragged breathing in the darkness. I lie down, facing the grave, watching the tiny shimmer of the moonlight reflect off the bracelet onto the granite.

Love you to the moon, Miranda.

I sleep eventually, and she comes to me in my dream. This time it's different. There are no skeletons. Miranda is dancing. Surrounded by moonlight.

And she's wearing the moonstone bracelet.

"Allow your true beauty to shine through."

—Torrey Grey, Beautystarz15

CHAPTER TWENTY-FOUR
MORNING BEAUTY SECRETS

I wake to the soft, hazy light of dawn. The moon is now a ghost of an image in the sky, and will quickly disappear as the sun grows brighter. I sit up slowly, stiff from sleeping on the hard ground. But I did sleep. All night.

Luis is sitting on the bench by Miranda's grave, looking at me.

"How did you know where I was?" I ask sleepily.

"Ross told me."

"Ross?" I'm surprised. "You talked to *Ross*?"

"Yeah. Ross heard Blair and Mia talking and told me what they were planning. When I got to the funeral home, you were leaving and looked upset," he explains. "I wanted to make sure you were okay."

"I'm sorry," I say. "For leaving you at the party. For taking them inside. For everything."

"I know."

"I was stupid." I blink away the tears.

He gets up slowly and walks toward me, sinking into the ground and gathering me up in his arms. We lie back down on the sleeping bag, my back tucked warmly against him and his solid arms wrapped tightly around me.

"You're not stupid," he whispers against my neck, his breath tickling down the inside of my collar. "Did you sleep?"

"Yes."

"Did you dream?"

"Yes," I say.

"You're smiling."

"How do you know?" I didn't even realize it myself.

"I can feel it. Do you want to talk about it?"

"Not yet." I snuggle back into his body and he sighs deeply.

After a while I do start to talk. "I just wanted to make it all go away, but there is no magic cure for missing Miranda. I know that now."

Luis twists a strand of my hair around one of his fingers.

"If I remember Miranda, then she will never really be gone," I tell him.

"What do you remember?"

"I remember the snow day when we both kept getting stuck in the drifts in front of our house. I pulled her out and we laid flat on our stomachs on the top of the snow, breathing hard and laughing until we both had sore throats from the freezing air. She was" — I think — "ten or so?"

Luis is quiet, listening, and I keep talking. "I remember her first few steps. She was so little. I held her hand and her tiny fingers wrapped so tightly around mine I was amazed at her strength.

"I remember her first day of school, when she cried and cried because she loved school so much she didn't want to come home. I remember her giggle, her games, and her songs."

"Those all sound like good memories," Luis says, and we lie there a little longer in the middle of all those tombstones, watching the sun grow stronger.

"I remember how opinionated and outspoken she was. She never backed down."

"Sort of like you?" He taps a finger against my forehead.

I laugh in surprise. "No one's ever compared us before."

"You don't agree?"

I think about it. "Maybe."

"It's one of the things I like about you. You put yourself out there. Even when you know you'll be criticized."

"You like me?" I say, even though I know the answer.

"Yeah," he says, and I feel his lips move into a smile against my neck. "Did you figure out what to say in court?"

"More like what *not* to say."

He pulls away and looks down at me, his eyebrows raised.

"There might be someone else who needs to speak more than me."

He doesn't ask who. Maybe he already knows. "What else did you think about?"

"I think I need to take a break," I say firmly.

"From me?" he asks, and I laugh.

"No, silly." I roll over to look into his eyes. "From my vlog." I realize then that I don't need to post the video I shot last night with Blair and Mia in my room. I don't *need* to post anything anymore. "I want to spend more time in the real world. Face-to-face."

"I like face-to-face," he says. He slides his hand down my jawline, and then he kisses me gently. Once. Twice. Three times.

"I better get home," I finally say. "I don't want my parents to start looking for me."

Luis tugs me to my feet. While he rolls up the sleeping bag and takes down the tarp, I walk over to the grave to collect the *ofrendas,* but then decide to leave them where they are. I don't need them anymore.

But there is one missing. I search the dirt and the grass behind the grave, but it's not there.

I smile.

I am completely sure.

Somehow.

Someway.

Wherever she is.

Miranda has the bracelet.

BEAUTYSTARZ15 CHANNEL

Video Update, November 1

Hello, Beauty Stars. Long time, right?

I know a lot of you have wondered how I'm doing and I want to thank you for the kind words and thoughts after my sister's death.

No makeup or beauty tips today. I'm taking a bit of a break from vlogging. Don't worry. I still love makeup and fashion, but I need some time away from the spotlight. I hope you guys will understand.

Before I go, one final bit of advice. Maybe you'll find it helpful. I hope so.

I want to encourage you to look away from the mirror and turn off your screens. Seek out beauty in unexpected, new places. Maybe you'll find it in an exquisite new friendship. In your own family. And you might even find it hidden deep inside something indescribably ugly.

But you have to look away from your own image.

Or you might miss it altogether.

So that's what I'm going to try to do. For now.

"Be unique to build your fanbase." —**Torrey Grey, Beautystarz15**

CHAPTER TWENTY-FIVE
WHAT'S ON YOUR WINTER WISH LIST?

"I want January!" Raylene is yelling so loudly into her phone I expect everyone on the football field can hear. "It will start everyone's year out purrrfectly." She laughs loudly into the receiver. "Get it?"

I guess the person from the Huntsville *Item* got it, because Raylene hangs up with a satisfied grin.

I gather my windblown hair up into a quick ponytail, then zip up my hoodie and sit down on the top step of the bleachers next to Ross. Although it still mystifies me, he and Raylene have been inseparable since the party two weeks ago, and it seems to be working out great.

"Stu beat that Dalmatian by two hundred thirty-four votes!" Raylene exclaims. She pumps her fist in the air so enthusiastically that she practically knocks her new leopard-print beret off her head.

"Congratulations. Now let's see it," I say.

The football field is packed; everyone soaking up the beautiful fall weather. Everyone is practicing something —

track, football, band, cheerleading, and twirling. The twirling part is why Ross and I are here — to watch Raylene's newest and greatest routine. As of Monday, she is now the official alternate for the twirling line and must be able to perform at a moment's notice.

"Hurry up," Ross calls, stretching his legs out onto the bleacher in front of us. "I can't be late for practice."

Groups of kids are scattered out along the benches waiting to go to an activity, or watching friends. I even see Blair and Emily over by the gate watching Mia and the other cheerleaders working on a routine.

The day after Halloween, Blair called me and apologized for leaving me in the funeral home. I actually think she was sorry, but I haven't sat at the popular table since. My choice. Ross hasn't been sitting there, either, not since he and Raylene started going out. Sometimes Blair, Mia, and Emily look a little lonely at the exclusive table these days, but I'm sure they'll pick up some newbies soon.

Raylene positions herself on the track in front of me and Ross, feet placed carefully in position and baton in the crook of her arm. "Ready?" she calls.

"Yes," I say, impatient. "Go for it."

Raylene struts across the track in front of us doing a figure eight with the baton. I guess it's impressive, but what do I know? I look over at Ross and he's watching Raylene proudly.

"Now for the double leg roll. It's an advanced combination." Raylene lifts one leg in a marching stance, her toe pointed toward the ground, and rolls the baton over the top of her thigh. Catching it with the back of her hand, she raises her other leg and the baton seamlessly rolls across the top of the other leg. She repeats it several times and I watch in amazement as the baton twirls around and around her legs.

"She did it." Ross sounds just as amazed as I must look.

Raylene bows and he gives her a standing ovation, whistling wildly between two fingers.

"Wow," I say, stunned, clapping.

Ross looks out toward the football field and past Raylene. "Sorry, I have to go to practice, but you were great." He tramps down the bleachers to give Raylene a quick kiss, then jogs out toward the field.

Raylene watches him go, then turns back to me with a grin. "Still need to practice my two spin. I drop it every time."

"But you're getting better," I say. "I can tell."

"I'm thinking about writing a blog about being on the twirling line," Raylene says. She hurls the baton up into the air.

"Really?" I duck as the baton goes flying past my head and crashes into the metal bleachers.

Raylene retrieves it, then sits down beside me on the step, breathing hard. "Well, not really about being on the line. More about being an alternate."

"There's probably a lot of people who can relate to that," I say. I don't warn her about the trolls and constant criticism. She'll have to figure that out for herself. Besides, Raylene might just be able to handle it. Maybe I will, too, again, later.

When I'm ready. There's no rush. Since I posted my last vlog on November first, I haven't gone back to check on the comments. And the sugar-skull makeup tutorial sits unedited on my computer. Neither Blair nor Mia have asked me about it since that night.

"Just be yourself," I tell Raylene. "People will love you."

"You really think so?" she asks.

"Sure."

"Your friend Zoe's channel is really growing. She has a ton of subscribers," Raylene says, then makes a rueful face. "Sorry."

"No, it's fine. Good for her," I say, and almost mean it. Zoe's first beauty vlog went up last week. Raylene told me about it, but I didn't watch it. I didn't need to. I realize I'll probably see Zoe, and Cody, when I go back to Colorado soon for the court date. What will I say to my former best friend? Will I need to say anything? I think back to our phone call again. Maybe I can learn to forgive her someday.

"She has this snarky attitude that's like a magnet for all the haters," Raylene continues, still on the topic of Zoe. "You should read the comments. It's not pretty."

No thanks. Been there, done that.

Raylene bends over to retie her pink tennis shoes, then looks back up at me nervously. Like she's afraid of what I might say. "But she's kind of like a train wreck. You just can't look away."

"I can," I say, tilting my chin up a little. It feels good to say because it's true.

"Hey. There's Luis." Raylene waves, the silver bracelets on her wrist jangling.

Luis raises a hand and smiles in our direction, then stops to say hi to Ross on the field before coming up to join us. I never in a million years would have guessed it, but Luis, Ross, Raylene, and I have become something of a foursome. Luis and Ross are talking again. And somehow, the dynamic of our little group works.

I watch Luis coming up the stairs of the bleachers, the fall wind ruffling his dark hair, and realize I'm grinning like crazy.

"Did I miss the show?" Luis asks. He squeezes onto the metal bleacher beside me and I catch a breezeful of his cinnamony smell.

"I can do it again," Raylene says enthusiastically. She stands and gathers up her backpack and baton. "But you'll have to wait until after practice."

"Sounds good," Luis laughs.

"Bye," I say. We watch Raylene bounce down the steps and run out onto the track. "She's getting a lot better," I tell Luis.

"That's good. By the way, I have something for you," Luis says. He pulls out a white sack from the pocket of his gray hoodie and drops it between us. "It's from Mrs. Zajicek's service."

"What is it?" I ask.

"One less kolache than was in the bag an hour ago. I was hungry," he explains. "They're left over from the viewing."

"Yummmm . . ." I bite into a cherry-filled pastry and a white napkin flutters out of the bag. I turn it over to see the message, written there from Luis's grandma.

Have a good day, Torrey! See you soon. It is accompanied by a big yellow smiley face.

"Thanks," I say, the smile on my face an echo of the napkin. I love that I've been welcomed into Luis's family, with their sugar skeletons and all.

"No problem," Luis says, then leans in and tugs gently at my ponytail. "Hey, I like your hair."

I have a fleeting thought of Cody Davis. "You don't think it looks better down?"

Luis laughs, reaching for the half-eaten pastry in my hand.

"What's so funny?" I ask.

"It's like this." He holds out the kolache, turning it upside down.

"Yikes." I grab for it, hoping to prevent a cherry mess on his white T-shirt, but he takes a huge bite before even a drop of the filling falls.

"It really doesn't matter which way you look at it. . . ." He smiles at me, his brown eyes almost a caramel color in the bright sun. "It's still delicious."

I feel my face grow hot. I don't care that Blair and Mia are looking our direction or that my phone is inside my pocket, buzzing with an unread text message. I lean over and kiss Luis. His lips taste like sugar.

"You're right," I say, grinning back at him. "It's sensational."

SensorOnline

GRIEVING MOTHER CONFRONTS DAUGHTER'S KILLER

Published on: December 15, 3:15:20 PM MDT

Boulder, Colorado — The man who killed Miranda Grey while driving drunk appeared in court today to face the victim's family. The victim's sister, sixteen-year-old Torrey Grey, well-known on the Internet for her beauty and fashion videos, was sitting in the second row of the courtroom with her parents, Karen and Scott Grey, when Waters entered. Ms. Grey later stood silently beside her parents, while her mother delivered the victim impact statement.

Karen Grey spoke to the defendant, looking directly into Waters's eyes the whole time. "My daughter Miranda Grey was killed by the defendant," Mrs. Grey said. "While my family wished our grief to remain out of the public eye, I have learned there is nothing private about losing a child. Today, I could try and tell you about the pain and torment our family has endured, but there are no words to describe the nightmares, the tears, and the grief. You killed my precious daughter and our lives will never be the same, but we will not let you destroy our family. We will always have Miranda as long as we remember her, and you can never take that away from us."

Following the hearing, Mrs. Grey said she had some closure and was trying to move on with her life. She welcomed Waters's decision to accept a plea bargain and avoid a lengthy trial. Torrey Grey declined to comment and left the courtroom with her family.

ACKNOWLEDGMENTS

When my first novel, *Skinny,* came out into the world I had no idea what it would be like to garner a small slice of Internet attention. Struggles with body image, and particularly obesity, are lightning-rod topics for many. While most readers shared powerful personal connections to the book, some comments were directed toward me personally. It was unexpected and sometimes disturbing, but also became the inspiration for this book. I am so grateful to everyone for sharing their thoughts with me and, even more importantly, for reading.

My publisher, Scholastic, is amazing and this book is testament to the incredible team of talent they bring to each book they produce. This book would not exist without the loving guidance of my editor, Aimee Friedman. Her expertise is evident on every page and I am so extraordinarily blessed to have her in my life. Thanks also to my publicist, Sheila Marie Everett, and Jeannine Riske, Yaffa Jaskoll, Elizabeth Krych, Alix Inchausti, Jackie Hornberger, David

Levithan, Lizette Serrano, Candace Greene, and Emily Heddleson.

Immense gratitude also goes to:

Sarah Davies at Greenhouse Literary, for being a fantastic agent and caring professional. I am so fortunate to have you in my corner.

My writing family — especially Lorin Oberweger, Debbie Leland, Kathi Appelt, and the YAMuses (Veronica Rossi, Bret Ballou, Katherine Longshore, and Talia Vance).

Leah Barrett, for helping me grow stronger mentally and physically.

My wonderful team at Colorado State University's School of Teacher Education and Principal Preparation who help keep the dream alive — Karmen Kelly, Rod Lucero, Jodi Drager, Matt Wurst-Calgari, Juliana Stovall, Lamb Caro, Wendy Fothergill, Andrea Weinberg, Derek Decker, Cerissa Stevenson, and Mark Stevenson.

Karen (the Dead Cat Lady) and Greg Rattenborg for needed distractions and entertainment.

Jay for the laundry, dinners, housekeeping, and keeping me from jumping off ledges.

My father and my sister, Marty, for the foundation and support for all my storytelling abilities.

Miss you, Mom. Every single day.

"Hopeless. Freak. Elephant. Pitiful."

That's what the voice in her head calls her. But Ever is ready to shed her demons and find a stronger voice within.

"Deeply moving...addictive."
—Lauren Myracle, *New York Times* bestselling author

"Will strike a resounding chord."
—*Bulletin of the Center for Children's Books*

Available in print and eBook editions

SCHOLASTIC™ Scholastic Inc.

thisisteen.com

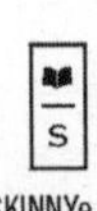

SKINNYe